*Xander followed Elfie as she almost danced down the path leading to the bright lights of the market and funfair.*

There had been something disturbingly intimate about posing for her, just the two of them in the dark. He could almost feel her concentrating on him, like a caress. He had stood there, barely able to breathe as she had explored him. Wishing he could explore her in turn.

He stopped, shocked. It was unlike him to lose control, even in his thoughts. And there had been no control in the image that had just flashed through his mind.

This unexpected attraction wasn't ebbing the more time he spent with her—it was growing. Maybe because the lonely child in him recognized something similar in her. Or maybe it was something far more obvious. He was a man who hadn't dated for a while, not since his father's last illness. And Elfie? Well, Elfie was pretty with extraordinary eyes and a gorgeous smile. Add full, kissable lips and a pair of the best legs he'd ever seen and maybe it wasn't a mystery why she had him in a spin. It was a simple matter of biology.

Dear Reader,

There is always a special magic about writing a Christmas book, about evoking those days of frost-covered rooftops, snowflakes and glittering lights, and this was no exception. And after the necessarily pared-down Christmas of 2020, it was a joy to imagine a Christmas full of traditions and romance set in a lavish Mayfair hotel.

Elfie has spent her entire adult life on the move, traveling the world as she flits between jobs, searching to recapture the safety and happiness of her childhood. Xander, on the other hand, has his life prescribed for him—protect the family legacy and ensure the family name is passed on. Both see Christmas as a season to endure not celebrate. But when Elfie is employed to look after Xander's temporary rescue dog, they discover that maybe Christmas is a time of hope after all—if they can just be brave enough to reach for it.

I had a lot of fun with Elfie and Xander—and of course with Walter the dog, whose resemblance to my own beloved pup is purely coincidental! I hope you do, too.

Love,

*Jessica*

# *Christmas with His Cinderella*

*Jessica Gilmore*

Recycling programs
for this product may
not exist in your area.

ISBN-13: 978-1-335-40689-7

Christmas with His Cinderella

Copyright © 2021 by Jessica Gilmore

This edition published by arrangement with Harlequin Books S.A.

For questions and comments about the quality of this book, please contact us at CustomerService@Harlequin.com.

Harlequin Enterprises ULC
22 Adelaide St. West, 40th Floor
Toronto, Ontario M5H 4E3, Canada
www.Harlequin.com

**Printed in U.S.A.**

Incorrigible lover of happy-ever-after, **Jessica Gilmore** is lucky enough to work for one of London's best-known theaters. Married with one daughter, one fluffy dog and two dog-loathing cats, she can usually be found with her nose in a book. Jessica writes emotional romance with a hint of humor, a splash of sunshine, delicious food—and equally delicious heroes!

## Books by Jessica Gilmore

## Harlequin Romance

### *Billion-Dollar Matches*

*Indonesian Date with the Single Dad*

### *Fairytale Brides*

*Honeymooning with Her Brazilian Boss*
*Cinderella's Secret Royal Fling*
*Reawakened by His Christmas Kiss*
*Bound by the Prince's Baby*

### *Wedding Island*

*Baby Surprise for the Spanish Billionaire*

*Summer Romance with the Italian Tycoon*
*Mediterranean Fling to Wedding Ring*
*Winning Back His Runaway Bride*

Visit the Author Profile page
at Harlequin.com for more titles.

For Rufus

And for all the Good Boys and Girls out there who have brought some happiness, companionship and much-needed exercise to their humans over the last year.

## Praise for Jessica Gilmore

"Totally loved every page. I was hooked right into the story, reading every single word. This book has to be my new favourite. Honestly this book is most entertaining."

—*Goodreads* on *Honeymooning with Her Brazilian Boss*

# CHAPTER ONE

'So, WHAT EXACTLY *is* the problem?' Alexander Everard Montague, Fifteenth Baron Thornham, eyed the so-called crack PR team he'd hired at great expense coolly, hiding his impatience as he waited for an answer.

The pause stretched, as if the two consultants perched on chairs opposite his three-hundred-year-old desk were playing some kind of game of chicken. The male cracked first. 'The problem, sir...' Hugo hesitated.

Xander steepled his hands and tried not to sigh. 'Yes?' he asked silkily.

Hugo looked at his colleague for support, but clearly none was forthcoming. She stayed silent, the serene half smile gracing her glossy lips unchanging.

'The good news is that the reviews for the hotels are uniformly excellent. The food, the facilities, the service. All five star.'

This wasn't a surprise. Xander worked hard, and expected the same from everyone he employed, ensuring that the hotels under the Baron Thornham brand were a byword for elegant luxury and peerless service. And he and they delivered. But in the last couple of years a certain *cachet* the hotels had effortlessly held for decades had begun to slip. Just a little, but noticeably if you were keeping a close eye on all the data—and Xander was.

To an outsider everything might seem business as usual, the hotels filled with the rich and entitled, every whim catered for. But Xander had crunched the numbers and he knew the truth: the waiting list was months and weeks rather than years and they were no longer the elite's first choice. Although still profitable and successful, the brand had somehow lost the exclusivity that set it apart from bigger, older rivals. And that exclusivity was their USP.

No matter what it took, Xander needed to fix it. Fast.

Healthy profits weren't enough. Xander wanted it all: financial and reputational success. The family name demanded it. The family honour demanded it. 'Do I need to repeat myself? Never mind the *good* news, what is the problem?'

Hugo gulped, straightening his expensive tie. 'It's you, sir.'

The word 'you' echoed around the study and Xander could have sworn he saw the portraits of his ancestors lining the panelled walls smirk in confirmation. He sat back, trying to formulate a response. 'Me?'

*You.* He could hear his father's frustrated sigh, the same exasperated sigh he'd give when Xander wanted to read rather than hunt, when he slipped away from yet another interminable party, when he struggled to make small talk with guests. No matter he had been a shy, bookish child, as a Montague the ability to command a room had been expected of him, should have come instinctively.

Xander's jaw set as he pushed the memories away. His father had never hidden his belief that Xander had been a disappointment as a son and as an heir. He would not be a disappointment as the newest Baron too. 'Explain.'

'Our research found that guests love your hotels. They love the feeling that they have stepped into the pages of a novel or a television show. The stately home, the Scottish castle, the Mayfair townhouse, the hunting lodge, the chateau, the...'

His mouth tightened. 'There's no need to list them all, thank you.'

He knew them by heart. Of course he did because, after all, the famous stately home in Buckinghamshire, the house in a discreet Mayfair square where he was currently residing, the castle in Scotland, the lodge in Yorkshire, the chateau in the South of France brought to the family by a French great-grandmother, the Rhode Island mansion, the legacy of an American buccaneering great-great-grandmother who had also bequeathed a charming Art Nouveau townhouse on New York's Upper West Side to the family, all belonged to Xander—to Xander and to whoever was prepared to pay handsomely to stay there.

Faced with high taxes and no income after the Second World War, his grandfather had resisted selling his property off, turning each house instead into a hotel where every guest felt personally invited, where dressing for dinner was encouraged and afternoon tea an institution, every day a house party complete with lawn tennis, croquet and lavish meals. And the potential of being personally entertained by a member of the illustrious titled family was the biggest draw of all.

Until now.

Hugo cleared his throat. 'Obviously your father and grandfather couldn't greet every single guest, but guests felt connected to them, even if they never actually met them. However, our research suggests that they find you a little more…remote.'

'Remote?' True Xander didn't have his father's bonhomie, his grandfather's easy patronage, but he had worked hard to overcome his natural shyness, to be welcoming. Or at least he thought he had. Clearly it still wasn't enough. 'In what way?'

'Guests feel as if they don't know you. That they're not personally hosted by you. And without that feeling of connection then the hotels are simply just hotels. Luxurious and exclusive hotels of course, but there's a lot of competition offering the same level of service, especially amongst your target market.'

'Luckily—' finally the woman—Pernilla—spoke '—this is an easy fix. We make sure your guests *get* to know you.'

'How?' Xander's forehead creased. What else would it take? Because if they didn't know him by now…

Xander had grown up travelling from hotel to hotel, never having a bedroom of his own, space that was his alone. His baby photos hung in the drawing room of Thornham Park, the family seat in Buckinghamshire, his graduation photo was displayed on the desk in the library at Glen Thorne in Scotland, his toys sat in the nursery here in London. His whole life had been on display, every meal taken with strangers, no family moment so private it was family alone.

Pernilla held up her tablet. 'Social media.'

'No.' Xander didn't need to think, his response a gut instinct; he didn't need even more of his life on display.

'*You* are the brand, *you* are the Baron, and when people book into your hotel it is as *your* guest. You are inviting them into your ancestral homes, to enjoy your hospitality. They need to feel personally connected to you.'

Much as he wanted to repeat 'no', send the pair of consultants back to their trendy Soho agency and demand a new strategy, Xander made himself absorb their words. Personally, he thought the agency name Milk ridiculous, found the consultants' style too knowingly quirky despite their semblance of formality, and he knew their fees were exorbitant, but he was also aware that their reputation was hard earned. If their research had identified Xander himself as the reason the hotels were losing their identity, then, uncomfortable as it might be, both the cause and the cure needed to be considered.

His grandfather and father might have died, but the need to prove them wrong was still very much alive. Xander had what it took to be Baron Thornham, to be the head of the family, to step into their shoes. It was time to prove it. To step out of his comfort zone, away from the spreadsheets.

'What kind of social media?' He braced himself against his desk, alarmed. 'Not the dancing one?'

'No, no, that wouldn't fit your brand at all. We were thinking visual. After all, you have the perfect backdrop. People want to see beautiful pictures of your hotels, famous guests enjoying the facilities, the food and all the décor, so much of it original. Show people your homes, your life, make them want to be part of it.'

Pictures. That didn't sound *too* awful.

'Let them see that the hotels are not just a short-term destination but a home you wish to share with them.' Hugo picked up the narrative. 'Whether that's through supposedly candid shots of you relaxing in an armchair in the library here, fishing in Scotland, playing tennis in Rhode Island or breakfasting on your personal Parisian terrace. Sell the Baron Thornham lifestyle through you, the actual Baron.'

'Through me. Right.' *That* sounded a little more awful. He wasn't really one for selfies. Not one for photos of him at all. 'I see.'

'We also thought—' Hugo pulled on his tie again '—that you might want to get a dog.'

'A *dog*?' Had he heard correctly? 'What on earth would I do with a dog?' Xander had never had a pet. A life spent moving around, regularly travelling across seas and oceans wasn't exactly conducive to pet owning.

'People love dogs—and, more importantly, they love dog owners. What better way to showcase the hotels and your lifestyle than through a dog? But time is of the essence. It's already the end of November and we recommend you launch the campaign over Christmas. We'll start with you choosing a dog to adopt from the local rescue, then spending Christmas with it as it settles in.'

Pernilla held up her tablet to show him a picture of a dog and its owner walking in a wood—an owner who had more than a passing resemblance to Xander. 'According to our research you usually spend Christmas Eve here in London before going to Thornham Park for

Christmas and Scotland for New Year. We tested that itinerary, with shots of a dog sleeping by the library fire, the two of you on wintry walks, the dog's Christmas dinner. Our test audience lapped it up.'

'It all sounds very winsome.' Xander was aware the words didn't sound like a compliment and he hadn't meant them to. The concept actually sounded like the plot of the sort of wholesome film he would immediately turn off. At least they hadn't mentioned matching jumpers. 'However, your research has missed one crucial detail. I don't know anything about dogs. I couldn't possibly manage a rescue dog.'

'We did take that into consideration,' Hugo said, a trifle too smugly. 'That's why we thought you should bring your dog nanny on board to assist you exclusively throughout the whole festive season.'

His *what*?

'Now her social media is really good,' Pernilla said. 'She has a lot of organic followers. The hotel itself plays it safe with its marketing, especially its social media, too safe in our opinion and we have a strategy to remedy that, but the dog nanny's account oozes with personality.'

'I employ a dog nanny?' Maybe he needed

an audit of every role in every hotel. Was there a cat masseuse and a hamster chef also lurking on his payroll?

'Three, actually.' Yes, Hugo was definitely verging on smug. 'One here in London, one in Paris and one in New York. Dogs are extremely popular right now with your core clientele, but they can be a hindrance in cities as most restaurants and entertainment venues won't allow them in. The dog nannies walk them, and dog sit if the owners are out for the evening.'

'Here…' Pernilla pushed her tablet onto the desk. 'Take a look for yourself.'

Reluctantly Xander picked it up and scanned the account she had selected. A vivid shot of three fluffy dogs, sitting on a checked blanket in the park, greeted him.

*Today's the day the teddy bears have their picnic! Meet Babe, Bear and Belle, contenders for the fluffiest dogs of the year award. Spending the afternoon with these three cuties has been an utter treat. Now it's time for theirs. Picnic-time, anyone?*

He swiped onto the next post. This time a handsome, slim dog sat posed before the fire in

Thornham House's library, a book open before him, a tweed kerchief around its elegant neck.

*It's raining cats and dogs outside and Austen is more of a bookworm than a hiker anyway.*

There were plenty more, all showcasing the hotel's canine guests out and about in the local vicinity or here in the hotel. There was no sign of the nanny herself, just the occasional booted foot or mittened hand.

'People like to read this?' He pushed the tablet back across his desk, unable to keep the scepticism from his voice.

'They do. She has a high following, excellent interaction and a much better organic reach than any other hotel account. That's why this is the perfect place to launch your social media and to kick-start the campaign. We suggest that she helps you choose the rescue dog and works with you while it settles in, chronicling it all on her account whilst you do the same on the one we create for you. She and the hotel will cross post you and we'll work with some influencers to do the same.'

This was really their strategy? A mutt and

some pictures? 'But the dog? It would actually live with me?'

'You have plenty of staff to walk it and so on after the campaign ends, if you didn't want to be bothered with that side of things. As long as your account still features it regularly.'

For a moment Xander felt pity for the putative dog, condemned to live on show, no real home, no family of its own, a prop and a marketing tool only. He knew what that was like. He opened his mouth, ready to send them back to the drawing board, when his gaze fell onto a portrait of his great-grandmother, dog on her lap, one hand resting fondly on it, and then onto one of a great-great-uncle as a boy, surrounded by spaniels. He'd looked at those pictures as a child and wished for a dog of his own every Christmas. But there had never been a dog under the tree for him; instead he would discover a fancy train set or a huge rocking horse. Expensive toys destined to be shared with any child staying here or at the castle or Thornham Park. His lips curled into a reluctant smile. He'd forgotten that old desire for a dog.

'Okay,' he said, to his own surprise. 'I don't have time to go to the shelter myself so get the dog nanny to select something suitable.

Something sleek, a decent size. A Labrador or some kind of hound. Nothing that would wear a bow.'

'Absolutely,' Pernilla said. 'Leave it with us.'

Elfie Townsend walked slowly down the concrete corridor, trying not to let her heart get pulled in a hundred different directions. It was an impossible task. She wanted to give each and every one a good home. The keen one with the bright eyes, wagging its tail enthusiastically. The excited one, barking as it danced around its door. The timid one, lying with its head on its paws, shuffling back as she approached.

But she wasn't looking for her own perfect companion. This was work. She had to find the kind of dog Lord Thornham wanted, a dog as aristocratic as he. Something tall, well-bred and aloof.

Easy.

The dog shelter was now Thornham House's official Christmas charity partner and so Elfie made sure she took plenty of photos of every dog she passed for both her own dog nanny account and the main hotel account. Their goal was that every dog here would find an owner by the end of the Christmas season and so every day she and the hotel's main account would post a picture of a different dog looking for a family.

'Aristocratic...' Elfie murmured as she stopped and took a picture of something small, white and very, very fluffy, imagining walking into Lord Thornham's study with that ball of wool under her arm and seeing his horrified expression. But no, she needed to keep her job until the New Year. She had decided against heading over to the Alps for her usual season working in the mountain resorts of the rich and famous, tempted by a lucrative offer to stewardess for a couple of private yacht charters in January instead. The last thing she wanted was to dip into her precious savings if she was unemployed for a few weeks.

'I'm sure somebody will love to give you a home.' She stooped down and scratched the small dog's ears. 'But you wouldn't want *this* home; it's not exactly cosy and you look like a cosy dog to me. Let me take your picture. I bet we can make sure you get a family for Christmas.'

She straightened, sighing as she did so. Helping re-home these dogs was one thing but, truthfully, Elfie wasn't sure she should be looking for a dog for Lord Thornham at all.

Her one encounter with the Baron had been short, to the point and chilly. Oh, she could see why some of her colleagues swooned over their boss; years of selective breeding had resulted in a face as finely sculpted as a Michelangelo. But although sharp cheekbones, a strong mouth and decisive eyebrows topping a pair of chocolate-brown eyes sounded dreamy in principle, the reality was very different when said eyes were piercing into her as if the owner wasn't really sure why he bothered employing her at all. What kind of dog would enjoy a life that seemed luxurious on the surface, but would potentially be starved of affection? She couldn't see the Baron rubbing tummies and patiently throwing a ball. What she needed was a nice, staid middle-aged dog who looked as if he or she would be at home in the pages of a hunting magazine and required little but a comfortable bed and regular meals.

Reluctantly, Elfie said goodbye to the small fluffy dog, promising again that he would be on the top of her list, and took another look around. The assistant who had welcomed her in had suggested that there might be a suitable dog at the end of the corridor, so Elfie headed in that direction, making slow progress as she stopped to acknowledge each dog with a murmured endearment and photo. She tried not to pause too long but found it hard to walk on when a grey, scruffy-looking dog sat up very nicely, lifting a paw to greet her.

'Why, hello.'

The dog gave the kind of yelp that could be construed as a hello back and Elfie took a step closer. 'Now, what are you?' she asked. 'One of the new design of breeds or a good old-fashioned mutt?'

Not surprisingly, the dog didn't actually answer, but tilted its head on one side in what she had to admit was a particularly endearing way. 'Oh, well, it doesn't really matter because, cute as you are, I wouldn't call you aristocratic. I'm not being offensive; I'm not aristocratic either. It's a good thing, makes us strong. But I am looking for a well-bred dog for a well-bred gentleman. If I had a flat of my own, a permanent job...' She shook her head regretfully. There was no point wasting time on what-ifs and if-onlys. One day she would be able to afford to buy her own home and then she would have a menagerie of pets. She glanced quickly at the printed nameplate. 'Nice to meet you, Walter,' she said. 'I hope we see each other again soon.'

Walter yelped again, rearing up onto his hind legs.

'You have all the tricks,' Elfie told him, backing away. Okay, maybe he would be top of her list for finding a new owner. It was hard; they all deserved one.

A few steps further and Elfie halted in front of Duke, the dog the assistant had mentioned. 'Hi Duke, you have the perfect name,' she said, holding her hand out to the handsome setter, but, to her consternation, instead of stepping forward, he shrank back, tail between his legs. 'I'm not going to hurt you,' she crooned, but Duke was clearly not reassured, retreating to a corner. Elfie bit her lip as she recalled the brief she'd been given. A hotel dog, a dog to be photographed, to be a social media star, to connect with the guests. 'I don't think you'd like that, would you?' she said softly. 'You need to be an only dog in a small, experienced family, not a publicity dog. I'll find you a good family, I promise. But not the Baron. You're not right for him.' Which was odd because Duke reminded her of Lord Thornham in some ways. She stood there, trying to figure it out. Both had haughty, sleek good looks, but that wasn't it.

Slowly, she went over every word of the very

brief meeting she'd had with him in the Thornham House study. He'd asked a few questions about her job, her social media account and then handed her instructions to select him a dog with as little emotion as if he'd asked her to pick up his dry cleaning.

And yet, behind the glacial manner, she had seen a glimpse of something she recognised. Loneliness.

Maybe finding him the right dog wasn't such a crazy task after all. Maybe a companion was something he needed just as much as every one of these dogs did. Or maybe she was just trying to feel better about the task at hand.

Either way, she had a decision to make and there was really only one way it could go. She just hoped she could talk him into agreeing or she'd be looking for a new job after all.

# CHAPTER TWO

A TENTATIVE RAP on the door broke the silence and Xander looked up, irritated at the interruption. He knew he'd been on edge for the last few days. Setting up his new social media accounts and deliberately putting himself at the forefront of the hotel's publicity had been an uncomfortable experience. An experience he knew was only going to get worse.

What on earth was he thinking? The hotels were turning a profit. Surely that was the only thing that mattered? He didn't have to try and be his father or grandfather. Didn't have to live up to their expectations, especially now they were gone.

But, at the same time, striving to be the man they had wanted, had expected him to be, was all he knew. There was no other path.

'Come in,' he barked at a second less tentative rap. The door edged open, followed by one of the hotel's porters. Xander repressed a grimace as he recognised Jon. The teenager was part of Xander's flagship apprentice scheme which trained local out-of-work youths in hospitality, but he seemed to be totally intimidated by Xander, which made every encounter excruciating.

Sure enough, Jon shuffled forward and addressed Xander's left shoulder. 'The delivery is here, sir.'

Xander raised his eyebrows. Matters like deliveries were not something that he usually dealt with. 'Shouldn't you be telling the chef?'

'No, sir. A delivery for you. For the new addition, sir.'

'Addition?' Xander frowned and Jon's gaze dropped.

'Yes, sir. I believe the dog is arriving today.'

Xander sat back and rubbed his temples, the nagging feeling of having made a misstep intensifying as the porter's meaning dawned on him. 'Surely you can manage to put away a bowl and a lead without my input?' As part of the PR package around the imminent arrival of the rescue dog, a local upmarket pet brand had agreed to additional sponsorship, supplying Thornham Hotels with all the paraphernalia any canine guest could need as well as donating food, toys and beds to the shelter.

'I think, sir, you'd better come and see for yourself.'

Xander stood up and stretched. 'Fine.'

He followed Jon down the corridor to the receiving bay at the back of the hotel. This was strictly staff only territory but there was no doubt of the season, with cheerful lights strung along the wide passageway. The decorations were nothing compared to the glittering display throughout the main public areas, all in the hotel brand colours of gold, crimson and cream, but they were festive enough.

'Here you are, sir,' Jon said with the air of a man glad to have handed over responsibility.

Xander stopped and looked at the stack of boxes in surprise. How much stuff did one dog need? 'What on earth is all this?'

'There are several dog beds in different sizes, coats, jumpers, toys, treats…'

'Yes, yes, I get the gist,' Xander said. It wasn't so much a dog he was taking on as an entire new lifestyle by the look of it.

'I was just wondering, sir, where to put it all.'

For once Xander didn't have an answer. He'd known that agreeing to taking on a rescue dog would add some complications to his life, but he hadn't realised quite how many. Possessions meant permanence, but how could a man without a permanent residence of his own supply that one basic need?

There were still too many unanswered questions. Where the dog would sleep, for a start. He had a preferred suite of rooms out at Thornham Park, but it was let when he wasn't there and he had no designated space here or at any of the other hotels. He usually took whatever suite was free, happy to move mid stay if needed. He lived on the move, travelling from hotel to hotel, country to country, packing lightly, used to living out of a suitcase, buying what he needed when he needed it. The only space of his own was the study he used here and its counterpart at Thornham Park. His had been no life for a child; it was certainly no life for a dog. The kindest thing he could do was put a stop to the whole idea. Tell—what was her name? Pixie? No, Elfie.

Strange name. It suited her, though, with her pointed chin and big grey eyes.

Eyes that had seemed to see through him.

Tell Elfie to forget the whole idea and charge the PR consultants to come up with a better plan. He didn't need a dog to make him seem human.

'Put it in the back storeroom,' Xander said, turning on his heel. He'd donate it all to the shelter. That was the kind of PR he preferred. Hands-off and philanthropic.

Xander returned to his study but, try as he might, he found it difficult to lose himself in the work that usually absorbed nearly every waking moment, pushing his laptop away to look across at the painting on the wall opposite—a painting of Thornham Park during the Regency.

Every painting at Thornham House was of an ancestor or of an ancestral home. A constant reminder of all that Xander owned and had to hold together. Not that he needed any reminder. He'd known his destiny and his obligations from the moment he'd first tottered across the ornamental lawn at Thornham Park. His grandfather had told him tales of ancestral heroes hacking their way across battlefields for war prizes and the honour of the Thornham name and every story underlined the same message: every blade of grass, every inch of polished parquet, every antique was entrusted to him to care for, to add to and to pass on.

Sacrifices were demanded of every Baron. He might not have to play political games at court or lead an army, but he did have to safeguard his heritage. Safeguard it and pass it on. His sacred duty.

Eventually, through force of habit and force of will, he managed to return his attention to the ever-pressing inbox and paperwork, losing track of time as he dealt with as many of the never-ending tasks as he could. He had no idea how dark it had become until a more forceful knock than Jon's recalled him to his surroundings.

Straightening his shoulders and flexing his aching wrists, Xander wished, not for the first time, that his life wasn't quite so deskbound and that he had more time to enjoy those acres he spent all his time preserving.

'Come in,' he said, and the door opened. He expected to see one of his managers with a query, or possibly a member of his waiting staff bringing him a coffee or snack. Instead, with a not unwelcome flicker of pleasure, he saw the slim, brown-haired woman whose direct gaze and pointed chin had made such an impression just a few days ago.

'Hello. Elfie, isn't it?'

'That's right. How are you?'

Xander stared at her in some surprise. He couldn't remember the last time anyone had asked him how he was. 'Fine,' he said automatically, without wanting to dwell on whether he really was fine or not. It wasn't the kind of question he'd ever been encouraged *to* dwell on. He had his health and his responsibilities, that was all he needed to know. 'I'm glad you're here,' he added, remembering his decision to cancel the dog.

'Oh?' She looked a little puzzled, and then her face lit up, her smile almost luminous with such infectious delight that Xander could feel his own mouth tugging upwards in a rare genuine response. 'Of course. You must be dying to meet him. It's such a big decision; I can't believe you delegated it to me. I hope you're pleased...' For one moment doubt clouded the glowing grey eyes before clearing, as if it had never been. 'You will be. How could you not?'

How, indeed? Xander had a sense of his legendary control slipping away. 'Pleased?' he queried, although he had a sickening sense that he knew exactly what she was going to say next.

'With your new best friend.'

His *what*? Xander had acquaintances and business rivals, contacts and partners, schoolmates and relatives, old lovers and occasionally new ones, but few friends, just a small close circle from school and university. It was hard to make friends when you were naturally shy and always moving around.

'You've chosen then?' Damn. He should have put a stop to this nonsense immediately. Luckily, it wasn't too late. He would just tell her to take it back where she'd found it and he'd make a nice large donation to the shelter. Everyone would be happy.

Everyone except Elfie maybe. But the happiness of one of his many employees wasn't his priority right now.

Although he would miss that smile.

'You are going to love him,' she said, her smile even brighter if possible, lighting up the room like one of the four huge, professionally decorated Christmas trees in the hotel reception. 'I guarantee it. I fell for him straight away. I can't wait to see your face!' She skipped back to the door and he heard her calling softly to something in the passageway outside. 'Come on, Walter.'

Walter? Like Sir Walter Raleigh? Xander's ancestors had once gone adventuring with the famous explorer. Maybe this was a good sign. Xander half rose expectantly, trying to ignore the unexpected hope fluttering in his chest, only to sink back down again as Elfie stepped back into the room, proudly leading something smaller than expected, knee-high at most, and covered with what could only be described as riotous grey fluff. She stopped a short way away and the mutt sat as she gestured towards Xander. 'Here you go, Walter. Meet your new daddy.'

Xander should have protested that he was certainly not intending to be known as any animal's *daddy*, but he was too robbed of both breath and words as he took in the medium-sized, at best, dog sitting by Elfie's feet. 'What *is* this?' he asked at last.

Elfie stared at him, a small crease between her perfectly arched eyebrows. 'It's the dog you asked me to get…' She faltered, looking a little less sure of herself. Was that guilt he heard in her voice, colouring her cheeks? He was almost sure it was.

'I asked you to get me something aristo-cratic, a hound.' He looked pointedly at Walter. 'Has this dog got any kind of pedigree?'

'It's hard to tell nowadays,' Elfie said. 'There are new breeds all the time. I'm sure he's got very distinguished parents on both sides some-where in his family tree.' She caught Xander's gaze and stopped, swallowing, visibly uncom-fortable. 'Look, I know, he's not exactly what you ordered, but I did think about this really carefully, I promise you. It's not just that he's cute, although he is; it's more that he's really good with people and he loves the limelight. Honestly, you should see him playing up to the camera. The one dog they had who fitted the brief you gave me was really shy. He'd be miserable living in a hotel, surrounded by strangers all the time, but Walter will love it.'

Xander had an unexpected pang for the unknown dog. Maybe they were kindred spirits.

'He's lovely, Duke, and deserves a really good home.' Elfie's smile turned reminiscent. 'I hated leaving him, leaving any of them, but it's amazing to know that the partnership between the hotel and shelter can help make the right home happen for him and all the others, maybe even in time for Christmas. I have to admit, I wish I could have adopted every one of them. But, for the kind of life you lead, the kind of life your dog will lead, Walter was the best one. It's working already,' she added, pulling out her phone, touching the screen and holding it out towards him. 'Just look at all those comments. He's only been on the dog nanny account for a couple of hours and already he's a huge hit.'

A hit? Xander wasn't sure he liked the sound of that. Because if the dog was a hit, then how could Xander send him back?

He took another look at the dog, who tilted

his head to one side and stared up at him, hopeful query in long-lashed, large brown eyes, and felt a faint tug of recognition, a connection. He pushed it away. He was a serious businessman, the last in a long aristocratic line. House pets in his family were for widows and aunts, or children in the nursery. Dogs lived outside and were trained as gundogs or sheepdogs or something else practical. There was no way he could take something that looked more like a miniature walking shaggy sheepskin rug than a noble beast around with him. He took a deep breath and tried to ignore the two pairs of trusting eyes fixed on him.

'This isn't going to work,' he said decisively. 'You'll have to take it back.'

Elfie stared at her boss, unable to hide her shock. 'Take him back?' she echoed.

The Baron nodded. 'I should never have allowed myself to have been talked into this in the first place. You're right, the life I lead is no life at all for a dog. Besides, I don't even want one.'

'But you can't!'

There was a long icy pause. 'And why not?'

Shuffling from foot to foot, Elfie considered her options. On one hand, she couldn't help but agree with Lord Thornham. If he didn't want a dog, then he certainly shouldn't have one. She spent far too much time looking after pooches who were pampered with exclusive diets and designer accessories but lacked routine and genuine affection. Plus travelling from hotel to hotel, country to country was no life for any animal, and she had heard plenty about how much the owner of Thornham Hotels travelled, how he had no house of his own, no home, his whole life dedicated to the family estate and the family business.

But, on the other hand, what was she to do with Walter? Already her post had been shared multiple times, including a couple of celebrities she had dog nannied for, and had gathered thousands of likes, the comments running into hundreds. The hotel marketing department had thrown a lot of money behind this PR campaign and the charity linkup with the shelter; if she returned the dog the negative press would soon overwhelm them. If she could see that, then surely Lord Thornham must. Which meant he must really, really not want the dog.

She tapped her foot, considering. There was another aspect, a less altruistic aspect to her instinctive refusal. Elfie served the ultra-wealthy simply because those clients tipped well, searching out jobs like her current one looking after the pampered pets of the kind of people who could afford to stay in one of the world's most exclusive hotels. Jobs that meant she could keep saving, helping her close in on her dream of buying her childhood home and finally having a place of her own.

She had a reputation for being diligent, hard-working and discreet. But if she was the one who returned Walter to the shelter then who would trust her with their pets or children or to serve on their yacht? No, she couldn't allow her hard-earned reputation to be devalued. She looked at Xander nervously; she couldn't help but feel he'd never heard the word *no* before.

'I'm just not sure it's a good idea, sir.' Understatement of the century.

Xander's eyebrows shot up; she was right, he *had* never really heard the word *no* before.

'Look,' she said, aware that she was sounding more than a little desperate. 'The adoption is already news. If you send him back, the fallout could be huge. People *like* dogs. And it's Christmas; you'd look like Scrooge sending Tiny Tim to the orphanage.'

But, with a sinking heart, she saw that he still looked determined. 'Scrooge didn't send Tiny Tim to the orphanage,' he said, and Elfie blinked. That was his takeaway from her impassioned plea?

'I know, I just meant if he had…' But she could see he wasn't listening.

'My grandfather told me to always follow my instincts,' he said. 'I should have done so this time. But it's not too late to put things right. We'll make a donation, a larger one. Get me the head of marketing in here and we'll come up with a plan to spin this disaster into something positive.'

Dammit. He meant it. 'I…' She wasn't quite sure what last desperate attempt to change his mind to make, different scenarios and arguments passing through her mind. She thought as fast as she could, letting go of Walter's lead as she clenched her fists and, before she realised what he was doing, the dog padded forward and disappeared behind the huge antique desk.

'Walter!' Elfie said quickly, holding out her hand, but all she heard in response was a deep sigh. 'I'm really sorry,' she added, darting forward to retrieve the errant hound. But as she reached the desk she looked down and stopped, hope returning. Walter had lain down, resting his chin on Lord Thornham's foot, his tail softly beating on the floor. He'd made himself quite at home.

And, miraculously, the Baron hadn't pushed him away. Instead, he was looking down at the dog with surprising softness in the usually hard brown eyes.

Hope filled her. 'Sir, you said yourself, when you sent me to get him, that he would probably only be here over Christmas and New Year, and that after that you'd send him to Thornham Park, where the staff would look after him. It's the beginning of December now, just a month to go. Please reconsider.'

There was a long, long pause, broken only by the thumping of the dog's tail. 'Very well. One month. Then he goes to Thornham Park and becomes someone else's responsibility.'

Elfie just about managed to stop clapping her hands together in gleeful relief. 'That's great, sir. You won't regret it.'

But his handsome face was still set in a frown. 'But I don't have time to look after and train him. You'll need to be looking after him full-time. Will that be an issue?'

Elfie thought regretfully of her lost tips as she shook her head. 'Of course not, sir.'

'Call me Xander,' he said unexpectedly. 'If we're going to be spending the next month together then you'd better call me Xander. And don't worry, you'll be handsomely remunerated for the extra hours. I need you to be on hand twenty-four-seven, living here for the next few weeks and then coming with me to Thornham Park for Christmas—will that be a problem?'

'No, I usually work Christmas,' Elfie said, more than a little dazed. Stay here for Christmas rather than in the tiny shared room she was renting in a hostel three tube lines away? 'It won't be a problem at all.' In fact, it would be very helpful. She'd let slip to her mother that for once she would be in the UK over the festive season and her mother had instantly started pressing her to spend Christmas with her. This way, Elfie had the perfect excuse to get out of it without upsetting her mother or being labelled difficult by her stepfamily.

'Then Scotland for New Year. After that we'll see.'

He nodded in clear dismissal, brows shooting together in query as she didn't move. 'Is there anything else?'

'I just need to go and collect my belongings,' Elfie said. 'But it's an hour's tube journey, so I can't really take the dog. What shall I do with him?'

Lord Thornham—Xander, she reminded

herself, his name feeling illicit in her mind—
looked down in some surprise as if he'd forgotten Walter was there. 'Take a hotel car,' he
said. 'The dog can wait with me. Be as quick
as you can.'

'A car, thank you. Yes, of course.' Elfie retreated quickly, holding in her squeal of joy. A
car to collect her belongings, a hotel room for
the next few weeks. This was turning out to
be the best gig she'd had for quite some time.
And so she'd have to spend more time with
Xander? He wasn't quite as forbidding as she'd
thought, and of course he was very easy on the
eye. Maybe this Christmas was going to be a
happy one after all.

# CHAPTER THREE

Elfie deliberately travelled light, and it didn't take her long to pack up her belongings from the small hostel room she'd been renting since her return to London. Luckily, the hostel charged by the night which meant she wouldn't be paying for a room she wasn't using.

Her limited wardrobe was functional, layers which took her from balmy summers in the Caribbean to the chill of an Alpine winter, and she had few personal belongings: an old, battered teddy, an e-reader, her beloved camera and the photo that stood on every bedside table, no matter which country she was in. She picked it up and studied it, her heart swelling. Three people standing by a lake, trees reflecting in the blue water. Her dad, young, smiling and so handsome, her mother, bohemian and relaxed, bearing no resemblance to the bustling, polished woman Elfie couldn't connect with, and Elfie herself standing between them, gap-toothed and grinning, no inkling that their idyllic life would ever end.

'Miss you, Papa,' she whispered. What would he think of this job? Would he have laughed and ruffled her hair and reminded her to keep it real? She'd never know. He'd died when she was twelve and she'd missed him every single day since. Missed him and their life together. Sometimes it felt like a dream, one of dappled sunshine, laughter and love. All she wanted to do was recreate that dream.

It was the height of luxury to be chauffeured back across London. December had set in, cold and frosty, sprinkling glittering white decoration on the streets and rooftops, Christmas lights sparkling in shop windows and strung up across streets in varying degrees of tastefulness. As they neared the hotel the decorations upped their game, money no object in these Mayfair streets and squares. And she would be right here in the very heart of it, part of the famous Thornham Christmas celebrations.

Once back at the hotel, Elfie had expected to be directed to one of the staff rooms in the attics but, instead of ushering her through the baize doors which still separated the staff quarters from the guest areas, she found herself led to one of the plush lifts which, like most of the hotel, combined twenty-first century technology and efficiency with a historical glamour that somehow managed to mix hints of Regency, Edwardian and Twenties luxury and still feel authentic. Possibly because the authenticity was real, dating back to when the building had been a family home used for the London Season, generations of redecoration and fashions melding together. During Christmas the Edwardian elements were at the fore, from the Christmas trees in every room to the rich, old-fashioned decorations, holly boughs on every mantel and greenery twisting through wooden banisters. The hotel smelt of spice and oranges, a hint of snow somehow permanently in the air. There was something magical about Christmas at Thornham House.

The lift doors slid open smoothly on the second floor and she stepped out onto the dark gold carpet. The porter took her two bags and carried them along the corridor, passing white panelled doors set into walls papered in cream and gold, heavy gilt-framed oil paintings hung between each door. Elfie followed, her footsteps silent on the thick carpet.

The porter halted outside a door at the very end of the corridor. There was no number, instead the oak nameplate read 'His Lordship's Chambers'. He knocked once, before opening the door with a heavy iron key—and holding the door open for Elfie to precede him into the room.

'Thank you,' she said as he placed the bags just inside the door, wondering if she should tip him when she wasn't a paying guest, and they were on the same staff. The solution came from an unexpected source.

'Yes, thank you, Franz.'

Elfie jumped at the deep masculine tones as Lord Thornham—Xander, she reminded herself—strode in, not through the main suite door but from a discreet door on her left, looking almost relaxed in dark denim jeans and a light grey sweater which clung to what she couldn't help noticing was a perfectly honed torso. She stood stock-still, unable to tear her eyes away for what she knew was at least several noticeable seconds until, to her relief, Walter, who had followed in his wake, spotted Elfie and dashed across the room to hurl himself against her legs.

'Hello there, boy.' She leaned down to stroke his ears, aware that her cheeks were heating up and horribly afraid they had turned red. She wasn't sure what was worse, ogling her boss or being so very obvious about it. 'Did you miss me?' She swallowed, trying to regain her composure, and straightened. 'He seems to have settled.'

'Yes.' Xander crossed the room to slip a folded note into the porter's hand. Franz smiled at Elfie as he discreetly backed out of the room and closed the door behind him, leaving her alone with Xander. And Walter. She was grateful for the dog's chaperonage as she looked around. She was in the sitting room of one of the hotel's famous suites. Two cream sofas faced each other over a low coffee table, a lit fire casting a warm glow over the crimson rug. A dining table set for four sat against the wall and two comfortable-looking reading chairs nestled in the large bay window. The door Xander had entered through was on the far wall, a second door on her right.

Her well-travelled bags looked incongruous amidst all this luxury. As, she suspected, did she. Elfie smoothed her jeans—dirtier, older and much less well cut than Xander's—and unzipped her puffer jacket as she searched for a rejoinder to his curt reply.

'This is nice.' Surely she wasn't staying here. Maybe she was looking after the dog while Xander attended some function and then would be shunted up to her expected place in the attic.

'Yes,' he said again, with as little interest as if she had complimented him on his car's valeting. Less. 'We had a last-minute cancellation which has worked out well. This suite is usually booked up throughout December but it's now free until Christmas Eve, when we leave for Thornham Park. Let me show you to your room.'

He picked up her bags as if they weighed nothing, although Elfie knew the exact opposite was true, and headed towards the nearest door. It led into a large bedroom, heavy curtains already closed against the evening gloom. A sumptuous-looking bed dominated the space. Xander set her bags down and nodded at a door almost hidden in the panelling. 'Your bath and dressing room are in there. Make yourself at home. Get room service if you're hungry, need a drink, anything. The staff know to charge any expenses to my account.'

'I…' She was staying *here*? In an actual *suite*? With food and drink on tap? Just think how much money she'd save. 'Thank you.'

'I've put the dog in with you.' His gaze

darted to a large dog bed by the wall. 'I trust that's okay.'

'Of course.' She'd share this room with a dozen dogs if that was what it took. The contrast with her hostel room, where she'd shared with three others, curtains around her bed affording her little privacy, her belongings kept in a locker, was stark. 'This is great.'

'My room is the other side. We share the sitting room but, as I have my office downstairs, I don't think that will be too much of an inconvenience.'

'No.' Hang on, back up a second. He was staying *where*? They were sharing a hotel suite? Calm down, she scolded herself. It was a suite, not a room. In fact, they had separate rooms, separate bathrooms; all they shared was a sitting room bigger than a sizeable flat. She need never see him. At all.

She slowly turned and took in the room. All this space just for her—well, her and Walter. She'd be a fool to pass it up. Besides, just three years ago she'd had to share a tiny cabin with one of the male deckhands when she'd been working on a charter yacht and she'd managed six weeks in a space smaller than this room's walk-in wardrobe without any problems. Of course, despite the deckhand's best attempts, she'd had little interest in him whereas Xander...

Okay. He was attractive. She couldn't deny it. But they had a strictly work relationship and she was a grown woman in control of her hormones. 'No inconvenience at all,' she said firmly.

'Great.' He cast a glance at her bags. 'So why don't I leave you to get settled in and then we can spend the evening planning our next moves?'

'Our next moves?' Either she needed desperately to cough or her throat had somehow swollen because she practically croaked the sentence out as if she were Mae West slinking over to bat her eyes suggestively at him. Elfie took a firm step back and folded her arms. There would be no moves. Xander was her boss. This job was too important to mess up just for the sake of a quick fling.

Not that any fling was in the offing. Look at him and look at her. He was a baron. Polished, sophisticated, aristocratic, and she was staff. She knew how to wait on and bartend, mind children and dogs and change sheets. They came from different worlds.

'With er... Walter.' He said the name reluctantly, as if trying it out for size.

Of course, Walter. The whole reason she was here. 'Yes. A plan. Give me five minutes.'

It was time to show Lord Thornham she was worth every penny of that generous reimbursement he had promised her.

Xander had no idea why he was so uncharacteristically nervous. This was just a business meeting after all, something he did every day. But Elfie, perched on the sofa opposite his, was nothing like his usual business contacts.

She'd changed into a short red dress teamed with black leggings. The bold colour suited her, warming her pale skin, accenting those extraordinary grey eyes. Eyes he was transfixed by—and that wasn't something that had ever happened before, not in a business meeting, not even on a date. And he didn't know what to make of it, of her. And that niggled away at him far more than he was comfortable with.

What *was* it about Elfie that discombobulated him? That made him want to find out more about her? To know who she was, where she was going, what had brought her to his hotel?

Xander had only dated women from his own background, potential future wives who were interested in his title and heritage as much, if

not more than Xander himself. And that was
fine with him; he liked the no-nonsense nature
of those relationships, knowing he wasn't expected to reveal anything about himself, that
he couldn't disappoint or be disappointed. Elfie
bore no resemblance to any of his past girl-
friends. She suited her name, slim and almost
otherworldly, with those huge grey eyes, her
heart-shaped face with its sharp cheekbones
and pointed chin, make-up free, her chestnut
hair pulled back in a casual ponytail. Everything, from the way she dressed, the way she
sat curled up in a corner of the sofa, to the
smile lurking in the dimples that punctuated
her cheeks, seemed so relaxed and devil-may-
care. It was alien to him. Exotic.

Alluring.

No. What on earth was he doing, thinking
that way? *Alluring?* What was he? A poet?
Only one Thornham had ever been a poet and
look what had happened to him. A duel, of all
ridiculous things.

He straightened, pushing all thoughts of
creamy skin and storm-coloured eyes determinedly out of his mind. 'Have you read the
PR strategy?'

Elfie nodded. 'Yes, and I have some ideas.'
She looked at him in query and he nodded for

her to go ahead. The consultants had been impressed with her, that was why they'd wanted her on board; it made sense to hear what she had to say. And both social media and dog owning were as alien to him as, well, actual aliens.

'This is all about your personal profile, so everything we do needs to look as authentic as possible. More, it needs to *be* authentic. Every post, every picture. I thought we could start with a walk around Hyde Park tonight, maybe a couple of shots of the two of you on the sofa...'

'Absolutely not. No pets on the sofas in any hotel.'

'We'll put a throw down,' she said soothingly. 'Then tomorrow a little bit of the same. Walter in your office, sitting at your feet while you work, maybe the two of you taking afternoon tea, sniffing round the gardens. Over the next few days we'll build in some Christmas shopping, sitting by a fire in the library in matching Christmas jumpers.' Her dimple flashed, hopefully to signify she was joking. Xander exchanged a look with Walter, a promise that neither of them would go anywhere near Christmas jumpers.

'That all sounds very reasonable.' Nothing too terrifying—or too personal.

'It's a good start, but we don't have long so it's important that we make as much of an impact as possible. After a few days warm-up we need to go all-in. You need to make a statement.'

That didn't sound quite so reasonable. He raised wary brows. 'A statement?' It was the hotels which made the statement, not him. 'In what way?'

Elfie clasped her hands together. 'I was thinking we should hold a Christmas fete—and include a dog show.'

'A *what*?' Xander wasn't sure what he'd been expecting her to suggest, but a dog show was nowhere on the list. 'Where?' Add in a *who* and *why* and he still wasn't sure he'd understand her reasoning.

'Here!'

'Here?' Had he heard her properly? 'The hotel is dog friendly, but only in certain areas and exclusively for dogs belonging to guests. I really don't think…'

'Oh, no, I didn't mean inside, but there is plenty of room in the gardens!'

Thornham House boasted the largest hotel garden in London, true, but she was still missing his point. 'Elfie, this is an exclusive hotel. People come here to get away from everyday life. This isn't a public amenity.' Especially not an amenity for the public's dogs. The lawn would never recover. 'We don't simply open our doors and let anyone in.'

'And you won't. This won't be open to just anyone, just local families and anyone who wants to come will need to register in advance. You'll know exactly who attends. Look, I was thinking this could be a charity event for the dog shelter *and* a way of involving yourself with the community. I was looking through some of your family history and when this was a private house, even in the first few years of it being a hotel, there was always a Christmas party for the local children. Your family held one at every property they owned. They were quite the event, with Father Christmas, presents for every child and their parents and a huge tea.'

That rang a bell. Xander had heard his grandfather mention it once or twice. Christmas was a big deal for all the Baron Thornham hotels, with family traditions at the heart of the celebrations. But, somewhere along the line, this particular tradition must have fallen by the wayside. 'And you want to revive it for *dogs*?'

'For local rescue dogs, yes. And local children too. Look, not everyone is a fan of the

Dog Nanny account; some of the dogs I look after are really indulged, they eat better than many families. I know a hotel like this is aspirational, is supposed to be out of touch, beyond day-to-day, but there's a limit, and a diamond-encrusted dog collar is that limit for many people. A revival of the Christmas party for local children tradition would be a way of addressing that, especially with a charity angle. It ties in perfectly with the PR strategy and the partnership with the shelter.'

'Dogs *and* children? You're sure that's all you want? It's Christmas, Elfie, winter. It's cold out. How much would it backfire if we ended up with freezing toddlers? It would be chaos. Besides, this is Mayfair. Any local child probably has a social diary busier than mine.'

Why was he even debating this?

But Elfie was clearly not giving up. 'You know as well as I do that there is poverty in every corner of London, and the joy of a community event is that it's open to all, whether they live in a mansion or a tiny flat. Invite your staff's families too. We could put a marquee up in the garden, sell those amazing mini mince pies and Yule logs the kitchen do, along with mulled wine, hot chocolate. Look. I know I just sprang this on you and it sounds a little crazy, but Xander, it could be amazing. It'll raise money for the shelter but, just as importantly, it'll show that you care about your hotel and the local community, about the charity you're sponsoring. It'll give you a presence online, yes, but beyond that too. Isn't that what this is about?'

Was it? Xander wasn't even sure why he had started all this any more. But both his father and grandfather had possessed the gift of making anyone and everyone feel welcome, no matter their background.

'When?' he asked warily.

Her eyes were hopeful and he could feel himself weakening, wanting, despite himself, to see that spectacular smile again, to provoke that smile. 'The weekend before Christmas, to give us time to advertise it.'

'I'll think about it.' That was as far as he could go. He got up, wanting to avoid the disappointment in her eyes. 'Did you say something about a walk?'

'Please do. We haven't got long, so if you want to go ahead we need to get started. But I appreciate it's a lot to take in.' Her voice was bright, professional. 'And yes, Walter's first walk is definitely on the itinerary. But first he needs his dinner; would you rather I take him to the kitchens or is he okay to eat up here?'

Xander's first instinct was to say the kitchens, but at the word *dinner* Walter had jumped to his feet and was regarding Xander with a hopeful expectation. He wasn't sure he could bear to be the focus of two disappointed looks in one five-minute period. 'Here will be fine.'

'Excellent.' She uncurled herself from the sofa and, caught off-guard, Xander found his gaze travelling up toned legs which, despite her diminutive size, seemed to go on for ever. The very air stilled, thickened, as his blood heated.

'I'll do it,' he said, needing to do something, be somewhere, to get his mind back in order. 'He is meant to be my dog after all.'

'Why have a dog nanny and feed him yourself?' Her smile wavered as he stared. 'Okay, that was funnier in my head. You know the saying, why have a dog and bark yourself? No? You're right, it makes no sense. Forget I said anything. Please. I'll get his kibble and bowl.' Her smile was flustered as she disappeared back into her room. Xander inhaled, long and slow. What on earth was going on? Why was he reacting to her every move like this? Standing and staring like an adolescent addressed by the girl all his mates fancied.

Not that he would know, having spent his adolescence in an all-male boarding school.

Actually, the why didn't matter. What did matter was how the rest of the month went. He might find Elfie attractive, but he didn't have to think about it, have to act on it. His goal was clear. Ensure the hotels returned to the very top of the most desirable lists, safeguard his legacy and then find a suitable Baroness and father an heir to pass it on to. A suitable Baroness who would understand his commitments, his sacred trust, his need to put the hotels, the land before all else. A woman born and bred to the position, just like his mother, his grandmother and every other woman who had borne the title—and subsequently an heir.

And that meant focusing on the campaign and not his new assistant's legs, quite apart from the inappropriateness, considering that he was, after all, her employer. Right. That was decided. Now he just had to somehow manage it whilst sharing a suite with her for the next few weeks.

It was going to be a very, very long month.

# CHAPTER FOUR

ELFIE PULLED ON her gloves and searched for something to say as they exited the hotel out of the discreet side entrance and started along the frost-covered, streetlamp-lit street towards the park. She wasn't usually lost for words; nearly a decade of working in the service industry and travelling meant she was a mistress of small talk, able to make easy conversation with everyone from billionaires to fellow backpackers who only had a few words of English. But Xander Montague, Baron Thornham was the exception proving her rule because she had nothing.

It was partly because he had been so lukewarm—at best—about her dog show idea. Which was disappointing because it wasn't a spur-of-the-moment idea; she had done some research and really thought a Christmas-themed charity fete would work and it had been nice, really nice, to flex her brain for a change.

Her mother always said she was wasting herself on a series of go-nowhere jobs. It wasn't that Elfie really cared what her mother said; after all, in Elfie's opinion her mother was wasting her own artistic talent. But to be told by an actual award-winning media agency how much they loved her social media account and inventiveness had been an ego booster she hadn't even known she'd needed. She was determined to do her best to make a real success of her part in the partnership with the shelter.

She was also reluctant to be the one to start a conversation after her attempt at a joke had fallen so flat. Yes, it had been an appallingly bad joke but the accepted polite response was for Xander to at least smile, not to look at Elfie as if he was about to dissect her, was trying to see inside her.

And that was the third reason for the uncharacteristic silence. Because, as she had got to her feet, she had caught Xander looking at her and if she didn't know better she would have thought that he was checking her out. Checking her out very slowly and thoroughly, those dark eyes moving up her body as if he were trying to learn every line. Her whole body had quivered as if he had actually been touching her. Worse, she had wanted him to be touching her, every nerve suddenly standing to attention. No wonder she had made a stupid joke to try and break the tension.

She must have misinterpreted the look. He was probably wondering what to have for dinner. Because why would a handsome, titled millionaire look twice at Elfie, small, scruffy and currently covered in dog hair?

'I'm really enjoying Hyde Park at Christmas,' she said in the end as they turned the corner and the bright lights of the winter markets became visible. As a conversational gambit it was better than nothing as Xander seemed content to walk beside her in brooding silence. It wasn't that Elfie minded silence, she didn't, but she preferred it to be comfortable, not stretch on and on. 'The lights are so pretty; I think it equals New York and they really know how to celebrate Christmas.'

Nothing. She gripped Walter's lead tightly. Silence it was.

'I like Paris.'

Had she heard right? A reply? More, a conversational gambit. 'Sorry?'

'At Christmas I always think Paris is very beautiful. Vienna too,' he added. 'But I don't own a hotel in Vienna.'

'Maybe you should, think of the afternoon teas. I still dream of the *kaffee und kuchen*.'

'You know Vienna?'

'A little.' She hesitated, not sure how professional to keep this conversation. 'My father was half French and I spent most of my childhood in France. Mum and Papa were both landscape artists, so we spent every holiday travelling around; they were looking for inspiration. A few times they pulled me out of school for a few months to spend time in different places—in Germany and Austria mainly. I remember Vienna really well, but I think that might mostly be because of the cakes.'

'That must have been an unsettling childhood.'

'Oh, no, I loved it. Papa always said home was when we were together, and we were always together. We'd stop the van, get out our cushions and rugs and throws and within an hour we could transform any apartment or cabin or house into a home.' Memories of places lived passed through her mind, different locations, different sizes and styles, but all full of love and laughter and for a moment she was so winded by grief and loss it almost floored her. She carried on hurriedly, pushing the emotion back. 'But there was something special about going back to our cottage again. It wasn't much, a little stone house that Papa always meant to extend and never quite got round to starting, but he and Mum chose it for the location, surrounded by orchards, with a river at the bottom of the garden…' Her voice trailed off and for one moment she could almost smell the blossom.

'I went to boarding school when I was eight, but I travelled a lot too, although always to our hotels, places that have been in the family for generations. The difference, I suppose, was that I didn't have a base to return to. A proper home.' There was a melancholy note in the last word that hit her right in the heart. She didn't have a home now, but she had once. 'Do your parents still travel around?'

'No.' She took a deep breath. The words still hurt. 'My dad died when I was twelve. We came back to England; Mum stopped painting and got a job and a year later she remarried. She only travels for holidays and, even then, mostly to their holiday home in Cornwall. No van required.'

'And you?'

'Me? I'm always on the move. I headed off the summer after I turned eighteen and I've been travelling around ever since. I started off waitressing in the South of France, thanks to my language skills, then headed to the Alps for the ski season. That led to a few seasons working on yachts, with ski seasons in between and backpacking in between.'

'And yet here you are. What brought you back to England?'

Elfie grinned. 'This is just temporary. Last year I was offered a nannying job in New York and did some dog walking on the side; when my visa ran out one of my clients mentioned this role and I applied. I've been here six months, which is a long time for me to be in one place. Originally I was going to head back to the Alps but I got offered a really good charter job in January so decided to stick around until then. This is the first Christmas I've spent in the UK for a long time.'

'Your mother must be pleased to have you around for once.'

She shrugged. 'She has a big family now; she knows I'm busy.' How could she say she deliberately kept away at Christmas, at all family occasions, popping back briefly when she knew her stepfamily would be away? That since her father's death she and her mother had grown so far apart it was as if they were on different planets, not just in different countries?

They stopped to cross the road and Walter automatically sat. She smiled up at Xander. 'He's got excellent manners; whoever trained him did a great job.'

'Do you have any information about where he was before the shelter?'

She shook her head. 'Apparently he was left on the doorstep with a note and his favourite toy. Someone who couldn't cope any more. It's really sad, because he was obviously loved. He seems secure, well trained, in good health. Look, I hope you don't mind me mentioning this, but I wouldn't be doing my job if I *didn't* mention it. I know you won't be looking after him full-time yourself, but he does need security.' She had known that the dog she chose was being offered a home for PR purposes, but she hadn't realised it was *only* for PR, how conflicted Xander was about having the dog at all. Walter had already lost one home; he deserved a place of his own.

'The manager at Thornham Park has one of the estate cottages and is more than happy to look after Walter when I am not there or when I am too busy.' Xander's reply was curt but Elfie was relieved to hear that he was one step ahead of her, that he had had the foresight to anticipate the dog's needs.

'That sounds great. As long as he's happy.' She'd known Walter for less than a day, but she was already falling for his scruffy charms. She didn't want to think about parallels to her equally swift but far more unsettling awareness of Xander, not that his charms were remotely scruffy. She stole a look at him as they crossed the road, tall and straight backed, black wool coat buttoned against the cold, a grey cashmere scarf wrapped around his neck, dark hair just long enough on top to give him a slightly rakish Edwardian air if it hadn't been combed neatly back. No, not scruffy at all, whereas her own coat was the one she used for skiing, a cream puffy affair, her hair pulled back because she hadn't had time to wash it. The two of them must look most incongruous together.

They reached the gate that led into Hyde Park. Ahead bright lights showcased the Christmas markets and the fairground. Instead, Xander turned down a quieter path, away from the noise and crowds, taking Walter's lead from Elfie as he did so. 'Doesn't it get lonely, always being on the move?'

She had thought the topic was over, the question catching her so by surprise that Elfie didn't have an answer ready. 'A little,' she said,

surprised into honesty. 'Sometimes. I like seeing the world, though; that's why I first headed
off. I wasn't used to staying in one place. I
missed the thrill of discovering a new region,
a new city, new customs and food.'

Well, that and her mother's second preg-
nancy. It had been bad enough living in someone else's house, feeling more than a little like
Cinderella with her two newly acquired stepsisters and their father, strangers to her in
every way. Her mother's first child with her
new husband had only made her feel further
estranged from this unwanted new family. A
second had cemented her position as outsider.
Better to leave.

'But you can't travel for ever, surely? You're
what? Twenty-five...six?'

'Twenty-eight.'

'What's next? If you keep moving on, then
how do you ever move up?'

'Not everyone wants a corporate future.'
This topic reminded her a little of her last
conversation with her stepfather. Actually,
it reminded her a lot. Defiant, she tilted her
chin. 'Not that I don't have ambitions. I have
a plan. I take jobs where I can live cheaply or
for free and get well remunerated. Stewarding
on yachts, chalet girl, dog nanny...'

'Dog nannying pays that well?' Was that a smile lurking on his well-cut mouth?

'It pays okay, I guess,' she allowed and was startled by his laugh. 'But the tips turn it from okay to pretty good. And I do have an end goal. My Papa always said that all anyone needed to be creative was time and place. He wanted to extend our cottage and turn it into a retreat for artists and writers. I want to make his dream come true. We still have the land, at least my mother does. I'm saving to buy it from her, to turn the place into the perfect artists' retreat. That dream makes every long shift, every difficult client, worth it.'

There was a long pause. 'I know something about family dreams. I'm sorry about your father.'

Her sigh was more than a little shaky. 'Thank you. And I know you lost yours earlier this year. It's not something that ever really goes away, is it?'

'No. Although of course I was an adult when mine died, and we weren't close. But I still want to make him proud. Even to the extent of getting a dog and agreeing to put photos of me with said dog all over the internet. Speaking of which, is this a good spot for our first portrait?'

Grateful for the change in topic, Elfie looked around. They were under a tree, a streetlight highlighting its winter-bare branches, in the distance the bright lights of the German Christmas market and funfair, the Ferris wheel silhouetted against the sky.

'This is perfect. Stand under the tree, look that way; that's right.' She was always assured with her camera, even a phone one, had been ever since her father had taught her how to properly look, how to frame a shot. She loved capturing a moment that no one else had witnessed, looking for an unusual angle. She focused more on the low branch and the wheel behind it, letting Xander and Walter almost blur into the background, taking a few in colour before switching to black and white. She then changed focus, zooming in on Walter first, posing like a professional, head held high and slightly tilted in an endearing way, before switching to Xander.

Her mouth dried. He was a photographer's dream, each sharp line, each hollow in his face creating the kind of angles a camera loved. He'd relaxed in the moments she'd been concentrating elsewhere, an almost dreamy expression softening the handsome face. She allowed herself the luxury of zooming in even more so that his face filled her camera, her gaze lingering on his mouth almost longingly, until the chill in the air reminded her she was here to do a job.

'Okay, that's good. Let's go and get some mulled wine and I'll take some less arty shots. It's always good to have a variety; each medium responds to different types of styles.' Speak professionally and she might act professionally. 'Come on, Walter, if you're really good there might be a bratwurst in your future!'

Xander followed Elfie as she almost danced down the path leading to the bright lights of the market and funfair. There had been something disturbingly intimate about posing for her, just the two of them in the dark. He could almost feel her concentrating on him, like a caress. He had stood there, barely able to breathe as she had explored him. Wishing he could explore her in turn.

He stopped, shocked. It was unlike him to lose control, even in his thoughts. And there had been no control in the image that had just flashed through his mind.

This unexpected attraction wasn't ebbing the more time he spent with her; it was growing. Maybe because the lonely child in him recognised something similar in her. Or maybe it was something far more obvious. He was a man who hadn't dated for a while, not since his father's last illness. And Elfie? Well, Elfie was pretty, with extraordinary eyes and a gorgeous smile. Add full, kissable lips and a pair of the best legs he'd ever seen and maybe it wasn't a mystery why she had him in a spin. It was a simple matter of biology, hormones and pheromones.

She was also his employee and that put her firmly out of bounds. Plus, now he'd turned thirty the next item on his to-do list was to look for his Baroness. Someone who understood duty, how to be a hostess, the importance of being custodian of an ancient estate. Love and attraction came a poor second to those requirements. But that was okay. Liking and compatibility was non-negotiable; he wanted a comfortable atmosphere, especially for any children, and desire would be a bonus, but he didn't require love. Maybe the expectation of it had been bred out of him by all those centuries of strategic marriage. Even his parents had married because they were a good match, his mother the daughter of an Earl looking for status and somewhere to use the unique set of skills she'd gained living in one of England's best-known stately home destinations.

No, it was too much to expect love *and* the kind of skills his future wife needed, he knew that—and the woman he eventually married would know that as well. It was a good thing he wasn't a romantic, had never fallen in love. It made duty so much easier.

And he was reconciled to loneliness after all.

But one thing was non-negotiable. No child of his would grow up lonely, always an outsider. Xander would do whatever it would take to make sure that didn't happen. When children came along, he would find a base for them, probably at Thornham Park. Work might keep him on the road but his children would have a home. And no matter their interests and personality, he would always encourage them to be themselves. To know that they were enough, just as they were.

By the time Xander caught up with Elfie and Walter they had reached the path at the edge of the fair. To one side were the rides. Families, young hand-holding couples and groups of shrieking friends thronged around the loud, flashing rides, the smell of candyfloss and excitement permeating the air. Ahead was the ice rink, music blasting, competing with the shrieks of the skaters, most inching gingerly around in the manner of the once-a-year skater, a few, more adept, speeding and spinning in the middle. Everywhere was noise and bustle. Looking down, he noted Walter pressing close to Elfie's calf, his tail down.

'It's too busy for the dog,' he said curtly, and Elfie nodded.

'Agreed.' She glanced over at the wooden shacks that made up the German market, just as busy as the other parts of the fair. 'But the light is good in this corner, gives the illusion of being in the middle of it all; we just need some props. Stay here, I won't be long.' She handed the lead to Xander and, before he could respond, disappeared off in the direction of the stalls. Walter whined, a short, pathetic sound, pulling on his lead and staring at the crowds now hiding Elfie from view.

'She'll be back soon.' Xander said gruffly. He wasn't used to offering comforting words. Commands, yes, questions, yes. But comfort? He wasn't sure where to begin.

Walter quivered, still straining at the leash. 'Come and wait with me,' Xander suggested, and the dog's ears pricked up. 'We'll both be more comfortable if you're not yanking at the lead.' He kept his voice conversational and was surprised at the thrill of accomplishment when Walter backed up until he bumped into Xander and sat. 'That's a good boy.' Crouching, Xander dropped his hand softly onto Walter's head. To his surprise, the wiry curls were soft. There was something soothing about the contact.

They waited there for a short time, breath cloudy in the cold evening gloom, until Elfie reappeared, carefully balancing a cardboard tray. The smell of fried onions wafted enticingly and Walter whined again, this time in hope more than misery, and she grinned, Xander's chest constricting as her face lit up once again.

'I've got a special onion-free one for you,' she said to the dog, setting the tray carefully down on the bench behind them. 'Just let it cool. No onions, raisins or chocolate for dogs, which makes Christmas a dangerous time,' she added, handing Xander a wrapped hot dog. 'Here, we didn't get dinner before we left. You're not vegetarian, are you?'

'Um…no.' He stared at the greasy bundle in his hand. He rarely, if ever, ate street food. But the hot dog did smell good.

'There's fries as well. But you need to earn your dinner.' Her phone was out again and she made Xander pose for a few shots, first sitting on the bench then standing with the fair lights behind him, before crouching and feeding Walter his onion-free hot dog.

'I'm not sure he even tasted that,' he said, stretching back up, and Elfie laughed.

'Me neither. Look at him, making up to you for more. You already had kibble, you greedy dog.'

Xander sat on the bench, unwrapped his hot dog and took a tentative bite. To his surprise, it tasted as delicious as it smelt, spicy and hot, the onions soft and caramelised. 'This is good. Thank you. How much do I owe you?'

Elfie sat down next to him and handed him the cone of fries. 'It's on me. Thanks to you, I am spending tonight in the height of luxury and I intend to make my way through the room service menu, so this is the least I can do. Here.' She reached into the tray and took out a sealed cup. 'Mulled wine. It seemed rude not to; it is a German Christmas market.'

'In that case, cheers.' Xander held his cup up to hers and she reciprocated.

'Cheers. To Walter and to a successful campaign.'

'To Walter,' he echoed. For a moment he had forgotten why he was here, why she had been photographing him. For a moment he had been a guy out at Christmas with a pretty woman and their dog. For a moment he had been utterly content.

# CHAPTER FIVE

'MORE TEA?' the waiter murmured.

Elfie sat back and considered her plate. She had rapidly demolished her half of the delicate smoked salmon and cucumber, turkey and cranberry, and brie and grape relish sandwiches, and had eaten both her savoury cheese scone—small, she reminded herself, practically doll-size—served with creamed Stilton, and orange and cranberry scone served with brandy butter.

She eyed the top plate of the three-tiered afternoon tea serving platter where tiny works of sugary art awaited her. Perfect mince pies topped with crumble or pastry, a mouthful of chocolate-covered Yule log, a square of stollen, gingerbread shaped into a Christmas bauble and delicately decorated. It all looked too good to eat. Well, almost.

'Yes, please.' She'd need the tea to wash down the cakes. It wasn't often an afternoon tea of this calibre came her way. She wasn't going to waste a single crumb.

Xander, sitting opposite, was far more measured. So far, he'd eaten merely two sandwiches and half his savoury scone. But, then again, food like this was an everyday occurrence for him, whereas for Elfie... She tried to suppress a sigh but failed and Xander raised his brows in query.

'You're not enjoying your afternoon tea?' he asked, and Elfie sensed the waiter next to her stiffen as if in alarm. No wonder when he was serving said afternoon tea to the man who owned all this luxurious decadence—and who was ultimately in charge of his job.

'No, the tea is delicious. It's all delicious. That's the problem.'

Xander leaned back, his mouth curved in amusement. 'I am struggling to see why.'

'Because I'm realising how easily I could get too used to this,' Elfie said, selecting one of the Yule logs reverently. 'Every morning I am brought a pot of perfect coffee with a miniature Danish, just to keep me going while I walk Walter. Then, after his walk, I come here...' she gestured to the orangery, with its comfortable sofas and crisp white tableclothed tables which doubled as the hotel's dog-friendly dining space '…where I order anything I want for breakfast. Anything. And then I sit in a comfortable armchair in the library and work on one of the social media accounts—did you know Walter is beating us both in terms of followers?—where I am brought lunch. And as for my room? That mattress is heaven. It's a good thing Walter likes a lie-in because getting up gets more difficult every day.'

Now Xander wasn't trying to suppress his amusement, barking out a slightly rusty laugh. It was rare to see him respond with more than a polite, mechanical smile and Elfie couldn't help feeling triumphant whenever she provoked a full-on grin from him, when he stopped being the serious and slightly stuffy Lord Thornham and became simply Xander. 'Are you complaining that the food is too good, or your job is too easy?'

'At some point I will have to go back to real life, and I don't know how I'll survive the shock when I am the one offering tea, not accepting it. Plus, if I carry on like this, I am not sure I'll even fit in my clothes come January, which for someone who has one carefully selected travel wardrobe is a serious issue. And yet I can't stop.'

'Isn't indulging the point of Christmas?' he

asked, and she shot a pointed look at his own barely touched tier of treats.

'For some.'

He laughed again as Elfie took a bite of the Yule log, closing her eyes as the intense chocolate hit flooded her taste buds, glad of the distraction. Sombre, work-focused, curt Lord Thornham she could handle, but her unexpected suite mate, the man she enjoyed making laugh, the one she was so aware of she could probably describe every millimetre of his wrists was another thing entirely.

No matter that she had her own bedroom and bathroom, sharing the hotel suite felt a lot more intimate than an anonymous bunkroom.

His laptop left on a coffee table, the book he was reading—he liked vintage crime, apparently—on a sofa arm, a bookmark denoting his spot. She saw him in his socks, in his post work version of casual, with his hair shower-wet and as he took his first coffee of the day. She saw the weariness descend at the end of another long, long day and noted how his schedule was all work and no play. Even his dog walks focused on work as she and her camera shadowed him, capturing as many moments as she could for posts, stories and the popular Walter blog on the hotel chain's website. She challenged herself to make him smile, and once or twice had found herself being gently teased in turn.

Then there were the charged moments... The times when silence descended and it was far from comfortable. The moments when she was achingly aware of every sinew on his forearms, his deceptively muscled thighs and the smooth planes of his stomach, the way his hair rebelled to fall over his forehead and the darkness of his eyes. The way he looked—or deliberately didn't look—at her. The heated caress of his eyes when he did.

He'd made no move beyond looking and nor had she. Here, she sensed, she was in charge. Xander was too aware of his position, his seniority over her to make a move. The power imbalance between them was all too evident. The bedroom she slept in, the food on her plate, that delicious morning coffee was all at his expense. And she was discovering that he was a man of absolute honour, that although his public image might be remote and austere, his staff loved him, especially those who had known him since he was a child, and he took his responsibilities to them very seriously. So no, he wouldn't make a move, his seniority, his rank, his title too much part of him.

Unless she was imagining the connection between them.

But she wasn't. There was no imagining the tingling sensation she felt whenever that dark hooded gaze was fixed on her, that absolute awareness of his every move, the way the very air stilled and thickened and their hearts started to beat together, a slow steady thrum.

Of course she could be the one to make a move. After nearly a decade of travelling and short-term jobs, Elfie wasn't shy about letting men know when she was interested. Time was too short in a ski season or a yacht charter to play coy games. What was the worst that could happen? A rejection? It was hardly going to compare with losing her family. She was happy to laugh it off and walk away with no hard feelings if she'd misread the attraction. But she didn't usually, her antennae were good.

But, no matter how good her antennae, she couldn't allow them to twitch in Xander's direction; not only was he her boss but he was also as far from her usual relaxed, easygoing type as a man could get. Quiet, thoughtful, clever and with an unexpected gleam of humour that warmed her through, he was a challenge, one she was increasingly drawn to solving. And that set off alarm bells. Elfie had never really fallen for anyone properly, never had her heart broken—or given it away. She wasn't about to start now, not when she was so close to achieving her dreams. Anyone who unsettled her as much as Xander did came with warning signs. She'd do well to heed them.

'Something wrong?'

With a start Elfie realised that she had fallen into deep thought and pushed all thoughts of attraction and love far away. This was the best job she had ever had. There was no way she was stuffing it up by allowing herself to proposition her boss. 'No, nothing at all. I was just thinking of captions.' She looked down at Walter, who was happily curled up at her feet, enjoying his own afternoon treat, a turkey-flavoured chew. 'I've got some great shots of Walter and you, and the cakes in the background look delicious so I'd like to draw attention to them; you can't beat a bit of product placement.'

'You're good at that. Have you ever thought of making a career of it?'

'What? Become an influencer?'

Xander winced. 'No. Do you have any idea how many try and blag free stays from us? I hate the very word.'

'But isn't that what you're trying to do? Influence the right people to come here, the kind of people who will make sure that this is the place to be?'

'In a way, but it's not as if we have a problem with capacity; it's just making sure we attract the right kind of people. It's about *who* wants to stay here, not how many.'

'Snob,' she teased, and that almost-reluctant smile warmed his eyes—and her body.

'I'm a Baron. It comes with the job. No, not an influencer, but a career in marketing. You have a good eye and a way with words. Look at the buzz you've created around Walter—it's way beyond the PR team's expectations and that's down to you.'

'I can't take all the credit; Walter's naturally photogenic.' He wasn't the only one. Xander's photos were also catching more than a little attention and some of the DMs he'd been sent would make a sailor blush. 'But thank you. I'm really glad you're happy and it's working. but I don't want a desk job.'

'Because of your artists' retreat?'

She nodded, oddly touched he'd remembered the casual conversation from over a week before. 'That's right.'

'It's a lot to take on. We both know how tough hospitality is—will you run it single-handedly?'

'I need to build it first,' she pointed out as her phone rang. She pulled it out of her pocket, only to abruptly silence it when she saw her mother's name on the screen.

'Sales call?'

'Hmm? Oh, no, it was my mother. I haven't figured out how to tell her I am still in the UK. She's bound to start making noises about Christmas when she finds out.' She pocketed the phone and sat back in the chair. 'It's always an easier conversation to have when I am a plane ride away.'

'Christmas?' He sat back, face wiped smooth and blank. 'Forgive me, I hadn't thought. Of course you should spend Christmas Day with your family. Walter and I will be fine for one day.'

'They're not my family,' she snapped and then, seeing the surprise on his face, she took a deep breath. 'I'm sorry; I just mean that I'd rather work. Talking of which, photos of delicious cakes aside, the purpose of this meeting was supposed to be to discuss the dog show and we haven't even started. Let me pull up the schedule.' She might have confided her dreams to Xander but there were topics that were strictly off-limits to everyone, and her family—or lack of one—was one of them.

But if she was going to confide in anyone, she couldn't help wish it could be him.

Over the next hour Xander found his mind wandering away from the Christmas dog show and children's party, which was rapidly taking on a life of its own with lots of sign-ups and positive publicity about Thornham House reviving a much-loved tradition. Elfie and the hotel events team had done an excellent job. But the deep sadness that had flashed across Elfie's face as she'd stared at her phone, the bleakness in her voice as she had told him the caller was her mother stayed worrying at his mind.

Xander wasn't close to his mother, just as he hadn't been close to his father. His parents had liked and respected each other but they hadn't been in love. His mother understood land and obligation and the need to turn expensive estates into money-making businesses and his father had needed a wife with those skills. After Xander there were no more children. But the marriage had endured successfully enough until his father's death earlier this year, and if either of them had indulged in affairs they had been discreet enough for Xander to have no knowledge of them. Not all his school friends had been so fortunate.

Since Xander had left university and taken on more and more responsibility for the hotels, his mother had become less involved with the UK and US operations, preferring to spend her time in France, either at the Paris hotel or the villa on the south coast, where she continued to be the consummate hostess, still playing her part for the family business. They weren't close; how could they be? But there was no animosity or dislike between them, quite the opposite; he supposed they were quietly fond of each other. If she had called with no prior arrangement Xander would have been surprised, but he would certainly have taken the call, and he liked to see her when their paths crossed. It wasn't family as some people knew it, wasn't close or warm or loving and it wasn't what he would want for any child of his, but it was theirs.

But Elfie didn't even have that, or so it seemed.

'And so, at the end we'll dress you up as Father Christmas and arrange for a sleigh pulled by Walter to fly over the garden.' Elfie looked at him expectantly, pen poised.

He nodded on autopilot. 'Okay. Sounds... hang on, what?'

'I knew you weren't listening.' She sat back and folded her arms smugly. 'I should have got you to double my pay.'

'Sorry, my mind was elsewhere for a moment. This all looks good, though. Thank you, Elfie. Restarting the Christmas party is an excellent idea; the Thornham experience is supposed to be about tradition, about a glimpse into an idealised version of family life in times gone by. It's a shame this particular custom died out.'

'I know. Without those traditions Christmas just isn't the same. Don't you think?'

Xander could hear a wistfulness in Elfie's voice, strange for a girl who always spent Christmas working by choice. 'Exactly, tradition is paramount. Christmas is the most popular time of the year because we make every guest feel like they're invited to our family Christmas, whether here, New York or Paris. We're often booked up years in advance, with a lot of repeat guests.'

'The famous Thornham Christmas. I'm looking forward to it.'

'It's pretty full-on,' he warned her. 'Christmas always follows the same pattern. A carol service here on Christmas Eve, followed by a special afternoon tea, then I drive to Thornham Park for the Christmas Eve ball and Christmas Day itself. Boxing Day is spent at Thornham Lodge for a nature walk, followed by a buffet of turkey soup, game pie and cheese and an evening of traditional games—it's the smallest of all the hotels; we usually have just one or two large family groups booking there. Then sometimes I head to New York for the week between Christmas and New Year, but of course New Year is spent in Scotland.'

A realisation he had been resolutely ignoring hit him. His father had been ill for the last two Christmases, battling the cancer that would eventually take his life, but had always rallied in December, his love of playing the consummate host giving him the strength needed for the strenuous two weeks of bonhomie. This year Xander would have no one to hide behind, the success of the season resting on him alone. 'Of course, this year it will be just me for the first time. My mother has chosen to stay in France.'

'You, me and Walter, although we'll have to sit New York out. He doesn't have a passport.'

Elfie's matter-of-fact statement warmed Xander, like unexpected colour in a grey landscape. 'New York is every other year, and I was there last year so no sitting out needed.'

'I hope there will be *some* sitting; you're right, that is full-on! When do you get family time during all that hosting?'

'Christmas was nothing *but* family time. We were all together, my grandparents, parents and me through the whole season. It was probably the only time in the year we were all in the same place.'

'And you got time just for you? For stockings and presents?'

He shook his head. 'Stocking hung in the Great Hall to be opened at breakfast with the guests, presents under the tree in the Sitting Room and handed out after Christmas dinner, also with the guests.' That was life as a Montague. Always on display.

'But...' Xander glanced up to see Elfie's hand half cover her mouth, her eyes huge and filled with unwanted sympathy. 'Even when you were little?'

'Even then. That's the promise, Elfie, a traditional country house Christmas, hosted by the owner. And we have delivered for over fifty years. Why so surprised? You work Christmas too.'

'As an adult. By choice. But as a child? As a child Christmas really was magical.' Her eyes softened, her expression dreamy. 'I told you my father was half French, and of course we lived over there, so we had a combination Anglo-French Christmas. It was chockfull of special family traditions, and we never missed one.'

'That sounds fun.'

'Oh, it was. Fun and lengthy. Christmas is a month of celebration on the Continent, and we took full advantage.'

'In what way?' He really wanted to know. To understand what brought the glitter of memory to her expression, the flush of remembered excitement to her cheeks. Even as a child, Xander had known that Christmas wasn't about him, his presents weren't necessarily for him alone. What *did* a magical Christmas feel like?

Elfie didn't answer for a moment, her gaze soft and faraway. 'We would start by getting out the Advent Calendar, a box with little drawers my father made me, each drawer filled with a little gift—beads, a tiny ornament, a hair slide, chosen with love. Then, on December the sixth St Nick would leave me some sweets and there was usually a party at school or in the village. St Nicholas Day was so much fun. I was too old for it when we moved back to England, but I missed it anyway.'

'We do a St Nicholas Day celebration in the French hotels. I've only been a couple of times, but they are popular. The French hotels have a tradition of exchanging gifts on Christmas Eve as well, which I could never understand as a child.'

'Oh, yes, we would open family gifts on Christmas Eve, after the most amazing feast, and then I would leave shoes out as well as my stocking. Our presents from Father Christmas would be left in those and sometimes under the tree as well, and then we'd head out for a walk before a traditional English Christmas dinner. We celebrated Epiphany too, with a special cake. It was weeks of happiness and laughter and magic, wonderful food and love. I know it sounds like a cliché, but it really was. Sometimes my grand-mère and grandad would be there, sometimes granny and grandpa, but I think my favourite years were when it was just us.'

'It doesn't sound like a cliché; it sounds wonderful.' Wonderful and alien, and for a moment Xander was hit with a longing so acute for the kind of family who made every occasion special, not because it was their duty but because of love, it hurt. He was greedy for more details, to live vicariously for a few moments. 'Did you have many white Christmases?'

'Oh, yes, not all but most. It was one of the

things I hated most about Christmas in Surrey, the disappointment of a grey Christmas when all I wanted was proper snow. I remember heading out after breakfast to go sledging, wearing the new hat and gloves Father Christmas had left in my stocking and knowing that I was the luckiest girl in the world.' She stopped, eyes shining this time not with memory but with tears and, prompted by a need to comfort her that overrode his intention to keep a proper distance between them, Xander reached over and covered her hand with his. Her skin was soft and warm, the feel of her a balm he desperately wanted more of. She didn't move for one long moment before turning her hand and lacing her fingers through his as if searching for anchorage.

'Thank you.' She tried to smile but it was tremulous. 'I don't usually talk about then; I try not to remember. It just hurts too much.'

'I guess it changed after you lost your father?' He kept his voice low, even and saw her start to regain control, the desperately lost look slipping from her face.

'Yes. He was the king of fun, my dad. He loved a party...everything was an occasion. Birthdays...' She shook her head. 'Birthdays were always over-the-top celebrations, starting with breakfast in bed—hot chocolate and pancakes, with flowers in a painted jug. I called it the birthday jug. But Christmas was his favourite time of all. We had so many family traditions—we always went ice skating every weekend in Advent, tried to see a version of *The Nutcracker* the Saturday before Christmas, went on a father-daughter present-buying day for Mum which included tea in a café. And then, after he was gone, all of that went too. It's like he was the heart of the family and without him we carried on, but all the happiness, all the things that made us unique, was gone.'

'He sounds like a wonderful man.'

'He was.' She laughed then, the pain in her eyes fading, replaced with nostalgic amusement. 'Oh, he wasn't perfect. When he was in the middle of a painting he could be really grumpy. And he could be really restless when he felt he needed a change of scenery, like this impending storm building. Mum didn't mind me missing school when I was really small, but she put her foot down when I was ten and said we had to stay put in term time and sometimes you could see his frustration at not being able to just jump in the van and go. But he was mostly full of laughter and so kind. But then one day he was walking along the road in the rain and a car took a bend too soon. And all that talent and love and personality was just gone. In a second. Mum couldn't cope and so we moved back to England, to my grandparents. And everything changed.'

'It must have been hard.' Their fingers were still interlaced, the feel of her pulsing through his skin.

Her eyes were unseeing. She was no longer talking to him but to herself, almost bewildered with hurt. 'It was as if everything I had been, everything we were, was washed away. Mum was an artist as well, not as renowned as Papa was, but she had some success. After Papa died she stopped painting, retrained in graphic design and got a job at a local business. Wore suits, make-up, had perfect hair, was always busy. And then a year later she married her boss. I thought she was joking when she told me. After Papa, how could she ever want to marry anyone else? So soon? But it was no joke.' The hurt intensified, her eyes bright with pain.

'Is he nice?'

She shrugged. 'I guess. We don't really understand each other; we never have. He was a widower with two girls, one my age, one older, and so we moved into their house. Mum didn't want them to feel like we were taking over, so she worked really hard to make sure nothing changed for them, especially at Christmas. No more St Nicholas or Christmas Eve presents; suddenly it was church services on Christmas Eve, their grandparents over for Christmas Day, Boxing Day at their aunt's. All our own special traditions were dropped. I put my shoes out that first year and they all just stared at me as if I was doing something really odd.'

'That's tough.'

'I was fourteen by then. Mum said it was time I grew up, but it felt like a betrayal. There was no time for ice skating or going to the ballet; instead there was a pantomime matinee and a trip out to choose the tree. Nice traditions, but not mine. Then two years later Mum had a baby, and I was really on my own. She was part of their family in every way, but I wasn't. I didn't know how to be. I didn't want to be.'

'Did she know how unhappy you were? Did you tell her?' The need to hold her, to comfort her was almost overwhelming.

'She thought I was jealous. That I didn't want to share her. She told me not to be selfish, that those poor motherless girls needed her too. But I had lost a parent too, and now I was losing the other one. Looking back, I just retreated into myself. I can see they thought I was moody and difficult. And life with Papa wasn't all perfect. If he hadn't sold a painting then we could be pretty broke and he left a lot of the household managing to her. There were a lot of highs and lows and by the time she met James I think she wanted stability, and he gave her that. Gives her it. She has a big house, two children and both my stepsisters settled nearby. It's a solid existence. Papa would have hated it.' She stopped, gently disentangling her hand from his, eyes fixed firmly on her plate. 'I'm sorry, I didn't mean to bore you with my family drama.'

'Don't apologise, and you didn't bore me. I'm sorry you had to experience that.' Maybe it was easier to grow up as he had after all, with distance and disappointment a constant, than having that distance enforced by tragedy and change.

'I know many have it worse. I have my memories, and I still do have Mum, just not in the way I used to. But Christmas is hard. That's the problem with having a perfect childhood. It makes adulthood hard in some ways.'

'You'll just have to recreate the traditions for your children.'

'I don't want children, marriage, any of it. Not when I know what it's like to lose it all. It's safer not to.' Her eyes were bleak. 'What about you?'

'I have to marry and have children. Otherwise, the title goes to a distant cousin who lives in Canada and has no interest in the hotels. He is as keen for me to procreate as my dad was.'

'Well, that's romantic.'

He laughed. 'There's no place for romance in my life. My parents married because my mother was bred to be a baroness and to help run an estate like Thornham, my grandparents too. I need a sensible wife with experience of this world, one who knows that work and the personal are always interlinked, who won't expect me to dance attendance on her, who doesn't mind us spending time apart and who understands the importance of an heir. This is how it is. How it has always been, whether it's my great-grandfather marrying a French heiress or his father marrying a buccaneer or the one before that the daughter of a viscount. The estate and the title have to be preserved at all costs.'

'But why?'

He blinked. He wasn't sure he'd ever been asked that before. 'Why do you want to build your retreat?' he countered. 'It was your father's dream, but why is it yours?'

'To remember him, as a legacy, I suppose.'

'Exactly. This is our legacy, ours and the hundreds of people employed by the hotel and the estates, some from families who have worked for us for hundreds of years. It's bigger than one generation, one man.' Xander wasn't sure why it was so important that Elfie understood his destiny, his intention. But for some reason it was. Maybe it was because he liked her, was attracted to her, maybe it was because she had confided in him and he had seen a little inside her soul. But, whatever the reason, there was no future beyond this month for them and he needed to keep their relationship purely professional. Even if his hand could still feel hers imprinted there.

# CHAPTER SIX

'OH, MY GOODNESS!' Elfie clapped her hands together, laughing. 'Look at them! This is the best idea ever. You're a genius.' If she hadn't heard him herself, she would never have believed that Xander had personally suggested a prize for best joint costume for dogs and their owners. The very idea of a dog show seemed incongruous with his usual dignified master-of-all-he-surveyed demeanour. But she knew him better now; ever since the afternoon tea a couple of weeks ago things had shifted between them—and in him.

Elfie still couldn't believe she'd been so open, so honest, had talked so much about herself. But that sense she'd had of a little boy lost somewhere beneath the poise and the command prevailed, even if he'd seemed to brush the label off, to deny any need for sympathy whilst offering it to her. And talking to someone who seemed to really, truly understand her had weakened her barriers, despite her vow to keep them firm.

She couldn't regret it, especially as, since that day, they had seemed to shed any awareness of rank between them and become friends. Elfie felt completely at ease around Xander, happy to pad around the suite in her pyjamas, hair tied back after a long day, to watch a film with him sharing popcorn, to tease him. They were the perfect flatmates.

Well, almost perfect because she couldn't deny the intense alchemy that still simmered between them and it took every bit of self-control she possessed not to act on it, to not react when his gaze lingered on her, intent and heavy and caressing. To see not the forbidding man she had first met but a handsome, desirable man who her fingers ached to touch. Every day it was hard to remember why that was a bad idea.

'I like that little boy's costume over there.' Xander nodded at a small child dressed as a red and gold bauble, his small, rotund dog in a similar costume. Both wore identical expressions of determination, scowling through long fringes.

Elfie laughed again. 'Oh, me too. And I

adore what that little girl's wearing, the one dressed as a reindeer. Isn't her lurcher gorgeous? I was chatting to her mum earlier and she said that when they got him he was still so skinny and so wary of people they had to tiptoe and whisper around him for the first few weeks. But now he's so relaxed and secure he doesn't even react to fireworks and he's been as good as gold this afternoon. Oh, and look at that small fluffy white dog, the one dressed as a snowball? I saw her in the shelter; I'm so glad she has a home already.'

'And I'm glad you talked me into this; everyone seems to be having fun,' Xander said. Elfie followed his gaze as he scanned the marquee, usually used for upscale weddings but today filled with the enticingly seasonal scent of mulled wine and hot chocolate. The display area for each round of the dog show took up the centre, ringed by chairs for spectators. Stalls set at one end served drinks or food and the dog shelter had been allocated space at the other end where volunteers were ready to talk to prospective donors and adopters.

A smaller marquee held local craftspeople, jewellers and artists, glad of a chance to pick up some last-minute Christmas sales, and the old stables had been turned into Santa's workshop for the day, complete with Father Christmas and a bag full of wrapped gifts. The air hummed with happy contentment. Upscale neighbourhoods like Mayfair didn't usually go in for community activities but a lot of families lived tucked away in the historic streets and not all of them were well-to-do. Anyone who had recently adopted a dog from the shelter had also received an invitation, as had all the staff's families. Some guests had even elected to come and join in the fun, and those who preferred not to had guaranteed privacy inside the hotel, the dog show and Christmas party a strictly outside affair.

The next couple of hours whirled past. Several journalists had turned up from local papers and from the kind of high-end magazines who liked to feature aristocratic bachelors in their pages and both Walter and Xander were photographed relentlessly. In between, Elfie made sure Xander was ready to judge each competition, award prizes and present the dog shelter with the sponsorship cheque. But in the odd moments when he wasn't needed for photos or presenting duties she watched him walking round the marquee, talking to everyone he met, admiring dogs and babies, quizzing small children on Christmas wishes and making polite conversation with adults of all ages. He was charming hospitality personified and all the chatter around her seemed to agree that he was a lovely man.

Pride filled Elfie as she took it all in. She had done this, had an idea and made it happen. Okay, she had had a lot of help; the hotel's marketing department, the events department, the kitchen, the grounds folk had all swung into well-oiled action the second Xander had sent his first exploratory email. But still. In just over three weeks she had created something wonderful. Maybe her dream of running her own retreat wasn't so farfetched; with this role she'd shown that she was more than a glorified waitress and nanny, that she had creativity and flare. Just like her dad.

'You're looking thoughtful.' Her skin tingled as Xander moved closer, his voice low and intimate, his breath brushing her skin.

'I was just thinking how much fun this is,' she half lied. She didn't want to sound big-headed and tell Xander that she'd been revelling in her own role in the afternoon's success.

'Thanks to you. I wonder how many other traditions have disappeared over the years? There may be other ones we can reinvent.'

'Only if Walter gets a starring role,' Elfie

said, leaning down to ruffle the fluffy head. 'He's loved being top dog today.'

'You definitely made the right choice with Walter; he thrives on publicity. I swear he knows his best side and the exact angle he needs to tilt his chin for extra winsome.'

'I wonder if his old owner will see the pictures.' Elfie straightened, that same jolt of sadness hitting her whenever she thought about what it must have taken to have given Walter up. This hadn't been a random thoughtless dumping; there had been a letter, a blanket, his favourite toys. 'What if he or she comes forward?'

'Then we deal with it when it happens. Maybe Walter would be happy if he could go back to his old home; as you said, he was obviously well loved.'

'Maybe...' Elfie squatted down and put an arm around the dog, not sure why Xander's matter-of-fact statement niggled her. He was right, surely. Walter would be happier with his original owner if it were at all possible. But she could have sworn Xander was becoming fond of the dog. He no longer stopped him from jumping on the sofa, sometimes volunteered for the morning walk and the other day she had come into the suite to find Xander in serious conversation with the dog about a planned refurbishment for the Rhode Island hotel. Would he really be happy to hand Walter over to someone who had dumped him, no matter the circumstances?

'Anyway, I wanted to thank you for today,' Xander continued.

'Just doing my job, boss.'

'This was a lot more than that and we both know it. I've asked Julio to dog sit and I wanted to take you out. If that's okay?'

*Take her out?* What did that mean? Although they had spent a lot of time together over the last three weeks they had always been chaperoned by Walter. Every walk, every meal had a purpose behind it, and was always work-related.

Of course, Xander could always want to discuss the next stage in the social media campaign, how this crucial week before Christmas would go, and start to make plans for winding down the dog-related content after New Year. He might even want to carry on the discussion about discovering other lost traditions, ask her to be involved. That was probably it. Although she could have sworn she'd heard a tinge of self-consciousness in his voice.

Elfie continued to hug Walter, burying her

face in his neck, not sure what her face would reveal if she looked at Xander, whether her inner fluster would be evident. 'Sure,' she said, her voice a little muffled.

'Great. There's a car coming at five-thirty; can you be ready for then?'

'Sure,' she repeated.

'If I don't see you before, I'll meet you in reception then. Good.' And he was gone before Elfie had a chance to ask about where they were going or what she should wear. Slowly, she got to her feet. An evening out. With Xander. Right then.

'It's a thank you,' she said to Walter. 'There's no need for me to go thinking this is any more than that. It's actually very kind of him.'

Walter's silence was, she felt, telling.

'I'm moving on in a few weeks and anything more than friendship would just complicate things. Besides, you heard him the other week. He doesn't do romance. He has a wish list for a wife and, apart from the fact I'm not looking to get married, I am pretty sure I don't tick a single one of those boxes. And that's fine.'

Walter put his head on one side and regarded her in a way that if he had been human she would have said was sceptical.

'Obviously I like him, and obviously I've

noticed he's attractive, but I like uncomplicated men and relationships and Xander is definitely complicated. Tall, dark and brooding is all very well in books, but not real life, don't you think? So a nice evening out as friends, as colleagues is perfect. I mean it; don't look at me that way.' With relief she saw Julio, the young Spanish assistant manager, making his way towards them, clearly wondering how he had been unlucky enough to have been picked for dog sitting duties. 'I'll see you later; we'll talk more then.' She handed the lead over and made her way through the now diminishing crowds back to the suite, mentally sorting through her limited wardrobe.

A travel wardrobe meant every piece of clothing had to be multifunctional, so Elfie had a couple of outfits that could be dressed up with some judicious accessorising. It was tricky, not knowing if she was going tenpin bowling or to a five-star restaurant, but Elfie did the best she could, matching her favourite green maxi dress with a pretty gold sparkly cardigan she had picked up in a charity shop earlier that week and her beloved boots. She added a long loop of gold beads and matching earrings before making herself up with more care than usual, frowning with concentration as she applied liquid eyeliner and several layers of mascara, topping the whole with a festively red lipstick. She didn't have time to do much with her hair so, after a liberal application of dry shampoo—the backpacker's best friend— she twisted it up, skewering it with hairpins and allowing a few tendrils to fall onto her face. Right, she was ready. Overdressed for bowling or anything physical, presentable for anything else. She hoped. She pulled a face at herself in the mirror.

'Be careful,' she told herself. 'This one is different.' It wasn't just that he was quieter, more thoughtful, more reserved than the men she usually was attracted to, it was the sheer force of that attraction, of her response to him. It was deeper than anything she had ever experienced before, and that was unsettling. He occupied far too much of her headspace already; she needed to make sure she didn't do anything stupid and let him into her heart as well.

Grabbing her coat, Elfie made her way down to the foyer, where Xander was waiting for her. He was still in the grey suit he had been wearing earlier—so probably not bowling then, she thought in relief—although at some point he had shaved and exchanged his white shirt and tie for an open collar blue floral shirt. He looked up as she walked towards him and his gaze heated. Elfie stopped a few steps away, unaccountably shy.

'You look beautiful,' he said softly.

'You scrub up okay yourself.' Which, as he spent most of his life in suits, was a good thing. Elfie was used to men who wore casual clothes, practical clothing as deckhands or ski coaches; she'd dismissed suits and the men who wore them as stuffy. But living and working with Xander had changed her mind, where one man was concerned at least. 'I'm not overdressed, am I?'

'You're perfect. Come on.'

A car awaited them and Xander held the door open for her before joining her in the back. She was still sure this wasn't a date in the strict meaning of the term, but it felt more like a date than anything she had ever been on before. No one had ever told her she was perfect with that degree of intensity before.

Elfie searched for something to break the silence that had descended over them. 'I hope Walter's okay.'

'Julio loves dogs; I'm sure they'll be fine. And he has my number in case there're any issues.'

'Mine too. I asked him to send me any good

photos from the walk.' She giggled, struck by the incongruity of their conversation. 'We sound like two new parents who have just left their baby with the nursery for the first time.'

'If I know that dog, it's Julio who we need to be concerned about. Walter will have him twisted around his paw in less than five minutes.'

'He already has.' Elfie handed Xander her phone so that he could see the photo the assistant manager had just sent her of the two of them in the staff lounge, Walter sprawling on a sofa, a nature documentary on the television. 'I don't think Walter misses us at all. Our baby is growing up!'

Xander was unaccountably nervous as the car deposited them at the small restaurant he had booked, just around the corner from Covent Garden. He'd wanted to give Elfie a treat as a thank you for all her hard work but, now they were here, he wasn't sure whether he'd overstepped. She'd confided in him, and he'd used that knowledge to plan the evening. Was it too much for a simple thank you?

But first, dinner. There was nothing too much about a simple dinner, surely. They'd eaten together many times now; he often joined her at breakfast or if they were tired after a long day they would order room service and eat together in front of a film, Walter snoring companionably at their feet—or at his side. He'd lost the battle of the sofa weeks ago.

But they always had a small, hairy companion to remind them why they were together. Without him the air felt charged, the evening full of intent.

Elfie looked a little puzzled as he held the restaurant door open, and he smiled as he saw her surreptitiously check the heavy man's watch she usually wore.

'It is a little early for dinner, but there's a reason,' he said, and her colour rose as she smiled.

'An early dinner just makes sure there's time for supper.'

The maître d' greeted them and showed them to a cosy table tucked away in a corner, so it felt almost unbearably intimate. Xander swallowed as he took his seat, all too aware that if Elfie, bare-faced and practical in her day-to-day clothing of battered jeans, was vibrant and attractive, this Elfie, made-up to showcase her remarkable eyes, a slick of red coating the curves of her mouth, hair up, emphasising the slenderness of her neck, was a force he didn't quite know how to deal with. Every exposed millimetre of skin made his pulse speed up, every smile or glance from those long-lashed eyes burnt through him. He'd never physically desired any woman so primally, so totally before.

Desired her, liked her, was challenged by her, interested by her, intrigued by her. More, she understood his work, and increasingly she seemed to understand him. The irony wasn't lost on him that in many ways she was his perfect woman personified—except that Elfie had dreams and aspirations of her own far beyond his world. And surely she deserved more than he was capable of giving.

She perused the menu with the enthusiasm she used for all food that Xander found so endearing. 'I never understand soup as a starter. I mean, in olden days to fill you before a scrag end of mutton fat and turnip absolutely, but soup is a meal in its own right. With bread, of course. Ooh, arancini and salad. That could be tempting. But will it leave enough room for pudding?'

'There's a pudding break scheduled later this evening, so enjoy your arancini.'

'Pudding break? Intriguing. And right, every night should have a pudding break scheduled in, don't you think?'

'Your evenings usually do, don't they?' He'd never met anyone with as sweet a tooth as Elfie. She was, he'd learned, a big fan of elevenses, afternoon tea and supper, in addition to the more usual three meals, and each of those involved cake or biscuits or some kind of chocolate.

'Guilty as charged. I think the chicken for a main. You? No, let me guess. The steak.'

'I'm that predictable?'

'No, but you did tell me once that steak was your go-to meal when you ate somewhere new. Unless this is the place where you bring all the girls?' Her dimples flashed as she shot him a teasing grin.

Xander's reply was interrupted by the waiter bringing bread before taking their order and by the time they were alone again Elfie had moved onto a different topic. Maybe it was a good thing. What would he say? That he usually wined and dined his dates at one of his hotel restaurants, that this little trattoria with its reputation for simple and plentiful food would be dismissed by the kind of women he dated, women who went out to see and be seen. That here with Elfie he was more at ease than he ever had been with any of them—and that he had no idea what to do with that information. No, it was a good thing she was back to discussing the dog show. Safer by far.

Five minutes later, with the wine poured, Xander found himself relaxing into the evening, the stress of the day finally falling away. 'This is better,' he said, almost to himself and Elfie looked up at him.

'You barely ate all day; you must be starving. Here, don't let me hog all the bread; it's ridiculously moreish.'

The bread did smell heavenly and Xander realised how hungry he actually was as he took a slice and dipped it into the rich olive oil. 'You're right, this is lovely, but I wasn't talking about food. More the absence of people.'

'I'm a person,' she pointed out.

'But you're restful to be around, you make it easy.' He paused, surprised by the words, by the truth in them.

'I'm not sure anyone has called me restful before.' Elfie took a sip of wine, her eyes fixed on him. 'Didn't you enjoy today? It must be odd seeing your hotel invaded like that. I guess it's usually a low hum of activity, not such a hubbub. The marquee was absolutely crammed at one point; it's a good thing we asked people to register, otherwise we could have been overwhelmed.'

For a moment Xander was tempted to do what he always did, to gloss over the truth. But in the last couple of weeks he had come to appreciate Elfie's directness, her honesty, and he realised he owed her the same. 'It's the hardest part of my role, working crowds like that, being on display,' he said deliberately and as he said the words out loud it was as if a weight lifted, the sharing of the secret easing some of the self-loathing he could never quite conquer. 'I find crowds, strangers overwhelming; at least I used to. Now I have taught myself to cope but I still don't enjoy them.' His laugh was humourless. 'I've learned to deal with hosting tables and entertaining guests, to play a part, I suppose, but I would never choose to put myself in that position. It's funny, I have no problem with management, with being in charge, with hiring and firing. I can address a conference or give a lecture, but small talk in situations like today can be like an endurance task.'

'It doesn't sound funny; it sounds difficult,' she said softly. 'Especially for a man in your position, where there *is* so much entertaining. If it's any consolation I would never have known you found it difficult; no one would. You looked completely at ease all afternoon.

Like you were born to rule, which I suppose you were.'

'Apparently so. Being on display like that is part of who I am supposed to be. My father, my grandfather, they revelled in it. All of it. The title, the guests, the pomp and pageantry. But I always struggled. As a small boy I'd hide in the library, under a table, somewhere quiet with a book. My father said I was his biggest mistake. That I had no Montague in me.' He shrugged, as if the words no longer bit. But they did. Maybe they always would. 'That he had no idea how he'd fathered such a dull son.'

'He had no right to say that.' She was all fire now, grey eyes blazing. 'Besides, you're one of the cleverest people I know. Watching you at work is almost daunting; your brain works so fast. In that conference with the States last week you were so far ahead they were like dachshunds trying to keep up with an Irish wolfhound! I almost felt sorry for them.'

Xander couldn't help smiling at the analogy. 'Ah, but being interested in the figures, in the actual managing of the hotels was never seen as crucial. The ability to hold a crowd with a story, to work a room, to flirt, were considered more important than doing the accounts; after all, we employed people to do that. Being rugby captain, riding to hounds, being at the front and taking every fence was more important than winning academic prizes. We got into Oxford through family legacy, not brains. My father wanted an heir in his own image, not a quiet, shy, bookish boy who grew up to prefer solitary sports like climbing to rugby, a few intimate friends to a large party, books to going out and getting hammered.'

'That shy boy sounds a lot nicer than the alternative. In my line of work I come across a lot of entitled men who absolutely love to go out, get hammered and then harass the help. Your father should have been careful what he wished for—and been proud of you regardless.'

'I don't know; maybe my father and grandfather were right. How they would shake their heads if they could see me now, needing a consultancy to brush up my image. To hear that the guests see me as remote. To see me fail, the way they always knew I would.' He took a gulp of wine, trying to swallow the bitterness. 'I'm sorry,' he said more levelly. 'This is supposed to be a fun night out. Let's talk about something more cheerful.'

'Okay, agreed.' Elfie nodded but her eyes still flashed stormy fire. 'But let me say something first. Okay, yes, you can seem a little aloof at first, but you know who else is aloof at first glance? Mr Darcy. And he is pretty much every woman's ideal man. You're a baron. No one expects you to be just like us; that isn't what anyone pays for. They want the whole smouldering, proud vibe. Take it from me, I've heard guests talk. I say embrace your Mr Darcy image.'

Xander set his glass down, almost choking on his wine. 'Getting a dog is one thing; there is no way I am swimming in a lake for any social media so you can put that thought right out of your mind.'

'That's the TV series, not the book, although never say never. And, secondly, there is no set way to do something, to be someone. No one who came today would have any idea you weren't enjoying it. You were the perfect host. I saw you talking to small children as if you cared about every sticky word, greeting every dog you passed and asking about its age and pedigree as if you were actually fascinated in the lineage of an ancient pug. You may not enjoy it but you have learned how to do small talk and you do it well. More importantly, your staff love you. Actually, they adore you, and I don't get the impression they adored your father in the same way. So you will be a different owner, a different baron? That's fine. You don't have to be a carbon copy of what came before.'

Xander stared at her, absorbing her fierce words. No one had ever said it was okay to do things his way before, had ever suggested there was another way. As much as he wanted to believe her, the idea was too new, too strange to absorb straight away. But, either way, her fierce defence of him warmed him through in a way he had never felt before.

Xander knew he was no coward, no matter what his father said, that facing down a crowd took more courage than clearing the largest fence. That getting his adrenaline rush climbing, not hunting was okay, having a small group of friends rather than a social whirl a valid choice. But how many of his choices, from the women he dated but had little in common with, to his decision to study business rather than pure maths had been done in a fruitless attempt to win his father's approval?

No one had ever told him it was okay just to be him before.

Tonight, he had planned a special surprise for Elfie as a thank you for all her hard work, but she had just given him something priceless in return. Validation.

It was a gift he would never forget.

# CHAPTER SEVEN

By THE TIME they finished eating and left the restaurant, Elfie was consumed by curiosity. It was only just after seven and she knew they weren't returning to Thornham House because she had been very clearly promised pudding later, which suggested there was more to the evening. The absence of a car to take them back confirmed her suspicions. Instead, Xander took her arm as they walked up a narrow road leading into Covent Garden. The gesture was almost old-fashioned, yet the light touch set every nerve ablaze, her body instantly springing to attention, hyperaware of his proximity, his breadth, his scent.

It was more than physical attraction. She knew attraction, desire. She enjoyed flirting, enjoyed a bit of romance, that sensation of realising she liked someone and that they liked her back, but it was always a fleeting feeling.

She'd never felt comfortable talking about her past or her deepest insecurities before—and she sensed that Xander was the same. Which was why knowing he'd chosen her to open up to felt more intimate than any kind of touch or act. He'd entrusted her with his deepest, darkest secrets. And with that knowledge she felt some of her resolve to keep Xander at a safe distance ebbing way. They were already way past friend zone, but how far this intimacy would—and should—go was still unknown.

One thing she did know was that if she could summon the ghost of Xander's father she would have a few choice words to say to him. Imagine having a brave, intelligent son and trying to change him into the kind of Hooray Henry who gave polo shirts a bad name!

'What's the plan?' she asked as they emerged into the famous square, now blazing with Christmas lights and thronged with evening shoppers and revellers. A huge Christmas tree dominated the space, colourfully festive. The lights, the excited chatter and the sounds of the brass band from the far corner gave her an unexpectedly Christmassy feeling, something that even the snowiest season in the Alps hadn't given her. And, to her surprise, even though she had spent the last fifteen years downplaying Christmas, finding this time of year too hard, she couldn't help but get that old anticipatory flutter.

'You'll see.' Xander was grinning now, his hand warm on her elbow, his steps brisk. 'In fact, we're here.'

'Covent Garden?' Maybe he had some late-night shopping to do?

'There.' He nodded to the huge building dominating one corner and Elfie blinked. She didn't really know London that well—a few shopping trips in her teens, some layovers—this year was the first time she'd actually worked in the city and she spent most of her time in Mayfair and Hyde Park. She scanned the shops, wondering which of them Xander meant, before her gaze alighted on a corner door with a sign over it.

'Is that…?' She turned and looked up at Xander, her heart suddenly so full she couldn't speak, eyes hot with tears.

He nodded. 'Our destination? Yes.'

'Really?'

'It's the Saturday before Christmas,' he said, smiling down at her. 'And you told me that Christmas isn't Christmas without *The*

*Nutcracker.* I wanted to put that theory to the test.'

'I don't know what to say.' She actually couldn't have said more, her throat too tight, her emotions suddenly raw and exposed and painful.

'You don't have to say anything. This is a thank you. For all your help, for your ideas.'

'No,' she said softly. 'I'm the one saying thank you. This is the nicest thing anyone has ever done for me. You have no idea what it means.' She stood on tiptoe and pressed a light kiss of thanks to his cheek, feeling him quiver under the caress. 'I'll never forget this.'

The next couple of hours passed by in a whirl of music and enchantment. Xander had secured sensational seats, facing straight onto the stage. Elfie was too overcome to really take in her surroundings or the other theatre-goers as they walked into the foyer and up the stairs, sitting in a daze until the conductor entered to applause and the familiar music began instantly transporting her back to childhood. She'd never seen this version before and sat wide-eyed as the party began and Clara received her Nutcracker doll before finding herself in a magical world of toy soldiers. As the first act came to an end, glittery snow falling down onto the stage, a choir's song soaring above the orchestra and what seemed like dozens of snowflakes pirouetted around the stage, the long-suppressed tears finally fell. How she'd missed this. How she'd needed this beauty.

Xander had pre-ordered champagne for the interval and they took their glasses up to the outside terrace overlooking Covent Garden and the lights of the city. Neither really spoke. Elfie was still too full of emotions she couldn't quite disentangle and the beauty of the ballet, whilst Xander seemed as brooding as the Austen hero she had compared him to earlier, his only comment that he was enjoying it much more than he had expected.

The second half was as wonderful as the first, with virtuoso dancing from the Sugar Plum Fairy and her Prince, both of whom fully deserved all the cheers and applause. Elfie held herself together during most of this half, absorbed in the dancing, but when Clara fell asleep, to be returned home, her tears started again, regret that the ballet was coming to an end mixed with grief for the naïve young girl she too had once been, a girl who, like Clara, found herself lost, in her case with no family waiting for her, no happy ending. But within the grief and regret was the realisation that she had been seen and heard. That right now, for the first time in a long, long time, she wasn't alone.

As the tears fell once more, Xander reached over and took her hand, his fingers closing over hers as if they fitted together perfectly, and Elfie held on tight, anchored by his touch as the curtains finally closed before opening again for the dancers to take their bows. Elfie reluctantly let go of Xander's hand to clap as hard as she could, the tears still flowing until the curtain closed for the final time, the lights came back on and people around them started to stand up and move. Elfie couldn't move, still watching the stage, the tears drying on her cheeks.

'Here…' Xander spoke softly, as if he knew she was still caught up in the magic of the music and dance. Elfie looked over and he leaned forward, gently wiping away the tears with a handkerchief, the tender gesture almost setting her off again.

'I must look a fright,' she said with a last gulp, her skin tingling where he had touched her, and he smiled.

'You look beautiful.'

Reaching out, she took his hand and brought

it to her cheek. 'Thank you. That was beyond magical. I don't think you could have done anything nicer for me if you'd spent a hundred years trying. I don't think anyone could. I've spent the last sixteen years running from Christmas and you have made it special again. Thank you.' She leaned into his hand, turning towards him as she did so, and almost forgot how to breathe as she saw the heat in his eyes. Heat and desire. Desire for her.

Just a few hours ago she had told herself that this was not a date and reminded herself that Xander was not the kind of man she could walk away from with her heart unscathed. The second of these things was still true but Elfie realised that she no longer cared. Whatever happened now, she was falling, had fallen, for him. Whatever happened now, she would have to deal with those consequences.

Elfie couldn't have said who leant in first, but one minute she was looking into Xander's eyes, still holding his hand to her cheek, the next his mouth was on hers, soft and sweet and intoxicating and perfect for a few precious seconds until someone exited the row behind them, the noise recalling her to their surroundings. She drew back, almost shaking with the emotion swirling through her.

'Thank you,' she said again, almost idiotically, not sure whether she was thanking him for the evening or for the kiss.

'The evening's not over yet.' Xander's eyes were no longer dark chocolate, his expression back to unreadable. Did he regret the kiss? Did he think she did? 'There's pudding, remember?'

The teasing note in his voice reassured her as she realised that any next step had to be down to her. That Xander was not the kind of man to take advantage of an emotional moment, that he wouldn't want her to feel that there was a price to pay for the evening. She could demand pudding right now and act as if the kiss had never happened and he would abide by that choice absolutely.

But that wasn't what she wanted. She knew that with every aching pulse. 'We could skip pudding.'

'No pudding? Are you okay?'

'I'm more than okay.' Slowly, deliberately she reached out and took his hand again, threading her fingers through his. 'I love pudding, as you know. But there are other ways to finish an evening.' To her relief the heat flared in his eyes once again although his voice was even.

'I don't expect payment, Elfie.'

'And I'm not offering it. But I do want you. And I think that you want me. And for all the reasons that it's probably a bad idea…'

'Like the fact that I'm your boss.'

'Like the fact that you employ me, yes. Like the fact that I am out of here in the New Year, and the very important reason that we have a developing friendship that I am starting to value very much and don't want to ruin. But, even considering all of those things, I would still very much like to see you naked.'

She could hardly breathe as she spoke as boldly as she could. It wasn't the first time she'd made the first move. But somehow this mattered more. For a man like Xander, a man who valued his privacy, his personal space, any misstep could change things between them for ever.

But what else could she have done? She couldn't ignore the simmering tension between them any longer, how she felt. How she was sure he felt.

It mattered. He mattered.

The silence stretched on and on, almost unbearable. Xander's face was still bland, unreadable, but his eyes had darkened almost to black, his jaw granite still.

Then, finally, just as she thought she might scream with tension, he spoke. 'Then what are we waiting for?'

The traffic was light and the cab whisked them back to Mayfair in record time, but every second felt like an hour. Xander hadn't touched Elfie since her proposition, but there was an awareness, almost physical, like lightning crackling between them.

Anticipation—or was she regretting her decision, trying to figure out a way to tell him she'd changed her mind? Maybe it would be for the best, Xander told himself firmly, even as every sinew in his body cried out in protest. He could kiss her now, take her hand, caress it, find that sweet spot behind her ear, on her throat, use every tool in his arsenal to seduce her, but Xander needed to know that if this happened—if they happened—then Elfie was with him because she wanted to be, not because he'd kissed all thought from her mind.

Not that *he* was thinking clearly. His whole mind, his body, every nerve and muscle were straining with the desire to touch her, to hold her, to explore and learn her. He'd never hungered like this before, and it was as terrifying as it was intoxicating. But he needed to remember two things. The first was that here she had to have all the power; his position as her employer made that essential. And the second was that she was leaving. Elfie was a wanderer and she had already stayed in London longer than she'd meant to. She didn't want to be tied down. It should be easy—he wasn't one for ties himself. But nothing was normal where Elfie and his response to her was concerned.

Maybe he should do the sensible thing and defuse the situation. But for once Xander didn't want to be sensible. For once he just wanted to feel.

Finally, the taxi drew up outside the hotel, one of the doormen hastening to open the door and settle the fare, as they walked through the hotel and travelled up in the lift, along the corridor to their door where, with not quite steady hands, Xander unlocked it and stepped back, allowing Elfie to precede him inside. The maid had been in to turn down, the curtains were drawn, lights dimmed and the champagne and chocolates he had pre-ordered awaited them on the coffee table. As Elfie took off her old battered coat and sat to unlace her boots, still not meeting his gaze, Xander opened the champagne and poured them both a glass, offering her one. She took it and downed it in one gulp and then finally looked directly at him, challenge in her eyes.

'So…'

'So,' he echoed, shrugging off his jacket and sitting down opposite her.

'You're a long way away.' Her dimple flashed and with her half smile the atmosphere lightened. They were friends after all, friends with an undeniable spark. This, whatever *this* was, was just a natural evolution.

'I just want to make sure that *you* are sure.' It took all his control not to stride over to the other sofa and pull her into his arms. But he'd just surprised her with the kind of highly charged emotional experience bound to weaken anyone's defences. She'd said this wasn't a thank you proposition but that didn't mean it was a fully consensual one, not if she was overcome by the evening and all it had stirred.

'Me sure? This was my idea, remember.'

'Oh, I remember,' he said slowly, deliberately and watched her pupils dilate.

'Well, then…' She took off her cardigan, watching him as she did so, and his breath caught at the curve of her arms, the exposed length of her neck. He'd never seen anything so alluring as the unveiling of her skin. 'My

point remains. You're a long way away.' Her
smile widened, eyes alight with mischief and
something deeper, darker, more potent. Something he recognised and thrilled to even as he
was aware that his control, usually ironclad,
was fast slipping away.

'Maybe we should do something about that.'
Xander stood, every movement careful, almost
languid, enjoying this anticipation. Elfie's grey
eyes were still fixed on him, luminous and
wide, her mouth parted, her breath coming
a little faster and the knowledge that her desire was for him awoke all his most primal
instincts. This girl was his, for tonight anyway, and he wanted, needed to make every
moment count.

He held out a hand and after a moment she
took it and he drew her to her feet, her skin
warm against his. She was petite, her head
barely his shoulder height, and a fierce protec-
tiveness enveloped him. She deserved happiness, for all her dreams to come true.

Xander couldn't give her the home she
longed for, but he could give her tonight. Not
that there was any degree of altruism in his
mind. He wanted, he needed this, her, more
than he could admit to himself.

Her gaze was fearless as he took his time

drinking her in. The proud tilt of her chin, the tendrils of hair emphasising her heart-shaped face, the curve of her full, lush mouth, until finally he dipped his head and kissed her. Light, exploratory, teasing; this kiss was just a taste. Their hands entwined, mouths barely touching, each testing out boundaries, seeing what the other was responsive to. Yet, for all its almost chasteness, it was the most intoxicating kiss of Xander's life. Elfie consumed him. The taste of her, wine and a sweet warmth that was all her, her hand in his, their fingers entwined in a caress which shot bolts of desire through him, the scent of her, delicate and spicy, like a Christmas treat.

She stepped closer, her other hand cupping his neck, and Xander could feel the warmth of her breasts against his chest, her hip against his, the line of her long legs. He curled an arm around her waist to pull her tighter still, the kiss intensifying as he did so, an all-in embrace as she opened up to him. Time stood still and all he knew was Elfie, the way her hand clutched at the nape of his neck, almost desperate, as if she were anchoring herself to him, the delicious feel of her warm body as his hand began a slow exploration, taking in the curve of her hip, the roundness of her bottom, before leisurely trailing up to the softness of her breast. She gasped against his mouth as his hand continued to wander, tracing the outline of her breast, grazing her taut nipple as he skimmed kisses along her jaw to the sensitive skin at her neck.

Step by step, kiss by kiss, he slowly manoeuvred her across the sitting room towards his bedroom door. He found the zip of her dress, easing it down until the dress slithered to the floor and she stepped out of it, bold and beautiful in just her underwear while she pulled at his shirt, undoing buttons with impatient fingers until she finally pushed it over his shoulders. Xander stilled for a moment as she explored the lines of his chest with her light delicate touch, her hands everywhere, each finger burning through him. Now it was his turn to unhook her bra, leaving that too on the sitting room floor as they finally reached the bedroom door and he pushed it open, his mouth still on hers, his hands taking their time to get to know every exposed, silky inch.

Finally, finally, they reached the bed and fell, in a tangle of limbs, onto the firm mattress. Elfie's hands had reached his belt and Xander hissed at the almost unbearable sensation as she eased his trousers down, kicking them off impatiently until mere scraps of material separated them. He sucked in a breath and pulled away, looking down at her. Her hair had come undone in their long journey to the bedroom and splayed out on the pillow, her eyes half closed, mouth swollen and lush. She was perfection from her small pert breasts to the swell of her stomach to her slim, long legs. He wanted to touch every part of her, taste every inch, hear her gasp and know that he was responsible for every moan.

'What are you doing?' she asked, eyes fluttering open, one hand reaching out to him.

'I'm just wondering where to start,' he said, allowing his gaze to roam over her, not hiding the hunger in his eyes. 'Here?' He kissed her neck, a light touch that made her quiver. 'Here?' The top of her breast. 'Here?' Her navel. 'Here?' The inside of her thigh. 'Any preference?'

She murmured something and he grinned.

'What was that?'

'All of it,' she said as his grin widened.

'As you wish.'

Elfie woke up with a start, stretching sore yet sated limbs, each ache a memory of the evening and night before. She'd never experienced anything approaching the intensity of last night in her life, had never felt so wanted, so desired, so seen, had never been so bold in articulating her desires or in searching out his. She turned and studied the still sleeping Xander. He looked different asleep, less guarded, more at ease with his hair tousled and long lashes veiling his cheeks. He seemed so innocent lying there, incapable of the deliciously wicked things he had done to her and with her. She shivered at the memory. Not just at the way he had touched and kissed her but the way he had looked at her, as if they had connected in every way, physically, emotionally spiritually.

There had been no discussion about what happened next but how could she go back to her bedroom on the other side of the suite and sleep there chastely, knowing what she knew? Knowing how he could make her feel, and how she reciprocated. She smiled smugly. The austere, aloof Baron Thornham falling apart at her touch, taking her apart in spectacular ways. A side of him hidden to the world that only she was privy to.

'Why are you looking so pleased with yourself?'

She hadn't noticed him wake and gasped

as he flipped her over, pinioning her with his strong body.

'Good morning,' he added, his mouth grazing her neck.

'I was just thinking about last night.'

'No regrets?'

'Not an ounce.'

'Good.' His mouth moved lower, and all thought disappeared for a long, long time.

An hour later Elfie had finally made it out of bed to shower and dress, curling up on the sofa with a cafetière of the hotel's delectable coffee.

She took a refreshing sip, reliving the night— and morning—as she did so. Who would have thought that Xander would have been such a practised lover? But, then again, why was she so surprised? He was rich, handsome, titled, successful, with that whole detached vibe that so often made women want to dismantle defences. He must have had potential lovers queuing up. With a quick, guilty glance behind her, she quickly searched on her phone. Xander Montague. Girlfriend.

A string of images flashed up. Xander, that cold look in his eyes which she now recognised as discomfort rather than arrogance, standing with an arm around an array of young women. He didn't seem to have a physical type beyond the kind of elegance that only money could buy. Some of the women were tall, some medium-height, blonde or brunette but they all shared the same type of double-barrelled surname, some with a Lady or Honourable tacked on. Interestingly, he didn't seem to have had any kind of long-term relationship.

'You look absorbed.'

She jumped guiltily as Xander walked into the room, his hair still wet from the shower but in all other ways back to the formidable Baron, suited and formal.

'Just doing some research.'

'Anything interesting?'

'Kind of. Actually,' she admitted, never happy with subterfuge, 'I was looking you up. Well, your romantic history.'

'Found anything interesting?'

She glanced quickly at him, relieved to see his mouth quirked with amusement rather than annoyance.

'Only that you usually date women called things like Figgy Fortescue-Delaney, with pedigrees listed as if they were racehorses. And never for very long.'

Xander poured himself some coffee and sat next to her. Elfie leaned in, glad of his proximity. 'Is this a *where is this going* conversation?'

'No, because we both know exactly where it is going. I am heading off after New Year.'

'I know.'

Elfie tried to repress a small stab of rejection at Xander's easy acceptance of the short-termness of their fledgling relationship although she knew how silly she was being. But for once it would be nice for someone to want her to stay. 'In the interest of transparency, my dating history is equally fleeting, although without so many convoluted surnames. I'm not judging or prying, just interested.'

'You have a right to be interested, Elfie. If you and I are going to keep sharing a bed, then you should feel free to ask anything you want to about where we stand and about my dating history.' He paused. 'Are we?'

'Are we what?'

'Going to keep sharing a bed?'

'Well…' she pretended to think about it '… I don't want to confuse Walter.'

'Obviously.'

'But if we explain it to him then I'm sure it will be fine.'

'Good.' He dropped a light kiss on her head, the brief gesture warming her through. 'Because I for one am very much looking forward to a repeat. Last night was spectacular.'

'Yes, it was.'

'But I also remember what you said yesterday. We *are* friends, and I really value that. You're independent and brave and kind and I can talk to you in a way that I have never really talked to anyone before. I don't want that to change.' He took a strand of her hair and wound it around his finger. 'I don't want you to feel that I have used you or lied to you, that this is some last wild fling before I settle down. I respect you far too much for that. I can't help thinking that if we were different people this could be the start of something really special.'

'Well, we are navigating co-dog-parenting together,' she said, wanting to provoke a smile, the intensity in his eyes unsettling her. She understood short-term and fun; she'd never had a problem leaving before. She couldn't allow this time to be different, not when her dream was in sight. Not when she knew how much it hurt to lose something—someone—she cared about. She wasn't a for ever kind of person. It was safer that way. 'But I value my independence, my freedom. I don't want to find it compromised by anyone. And you have a Baroness to find.' Xander might like her, value her, desire her, but he didn't want to marry her. 'Any contenders for that position?' Friends should be able to discuss these matters, even if they were friends with benefits, even if unwanted, unaccustomed jealousy clawed at her as she affected an easy tone and a smile.

Xander took a sip of his coffee. 'As you know, I see marriage has to be a practical decision. Things haven't changed that much since debutante balls and Seasons. People like me date, try each other on for size, look at what each partner brings to a marriage and if we're compatible we marry.'

'So that's what you've been doing? Trying these women on for size.'

'And they were trying me, along with other men in our social circle. We all know the score. Fun in our twenties, and now we're all approaching or in our thirties there will be a flurry of weddings. It's the way it's always been.'

'And you don't have a frontrunner?' She tried to sound light, interested, as if she wasn't jealous at the thought of some other woman sharing his bed, his life. Because that would be ridiculous.

'I wouldn't be here if there was. Elfie, what we shared last night was special. My marriage will be practical and that's fine, but I will always be very grateful I got to spend this time with you. Always.'

'It's not over yet.' She reached up and caressed his cheek, revelling in the feel of stubble under her fingers, trying not to dwell on his words, the unexpected disquiet rumbling through her. This was exactly what she wanted, a no-strings fling full of passion and mutual respect which left her free for her next adventure. So why did the thought of Xander marrying some unknown woman he didn't even love make her feel as if she couldn't breathe?

With an effort she pushed all thought away, pulling Xander close, letting her lips find his, losing herself in the sensation of his kiss. The here and now was all that mattered. Tomorrow could take care of itself.

# CHAPTER EIGHT

Xander walked into the Orangery to see Elfie surrounded by envelopes, laptop open, unusual frown lines creasing her forehead. 'What's all this?'

He wanted to pull her close, kiss her, but they were keeping their fling secret and this space was all too public. It was getting harder not to touch her, to tell everyone, *She is mine*, but Elfie didn't want their relationship to affect the other members of staff, especially when it was going to be so short-lived.

Too short-lived. January was less than a fortnight away. If Elfie hadn't planned to be going away then what would happen? Would they see where this went? Part of him could see it, properly dating, getting to know each other away from this festive bubble. But the rest of him, the sensible part of him, knew that Elfie was a free spirit, that the life of duty he led would eventually feel like a prison. Maybe it was better to have an end date after all.

She looked up, barely mustering a smile. 'These are all the letters and emails from people purporting to be Walter's owner.'

'*What?*'

She nodded. 'Over three hundred. There were several features about him over the last few days and so some enterprising con artists have decided that this is the way to make money. Some have asked for money in return for not claiming him, others have sob stories about why they had to give him up and have suggested that a sum of money ranging from several thousand to fifty thousand pounds would enable them to be reunited and keep him.'

'Fifty thousand *pounds*? His pedigree must be a lot more special than we realised.'

'It's more that they know you're a baron and that you own all this. I guess that ups the stakes.'

Picking up one of the letters, Xander scanned the long paragraphs full of woe. 'But what if one of them is genuine?'

'They're not; none have mentioned the squirrel toy left with him and that detail wasn't mentioned to any of the journalists. But I feel like I should check each one, just in case.' She laid a hand on Walter's head. 'For your sake anyway.'

Xander slid into a chair next to her. 'Pass me a pile of these. I'll help.'

'I thought you were busy?'

'I am, but this is important.' Although the thought of actually finding Walter's owner and possibly giving the dog back was far less welcome than it would have been a few weeks ago. He was getting used to his presence, to his sighs and snores, the way he bounded to the door at the word 'walk' to the way he sometimes pressed close to Xander for comfort. It had turned out that Walter was surprisingly good company and walking him was now Xander's favourite time of day. He'd even met several people with the same routine and would stand and make small talk while the dogs played. He had no idea of their names or anything about them other than the name and breed of their dog. It was refreshingly anonymous to be known simply as Walter's owner.

But, at the same time, the letter that had accompanied Walter had made it clear his previous owner had felt he or she had no choice and the small dog had clearly been well looked after and well trained. If his owner did get in touch then surely Xander was duty bound to try and help reunite them, no matter what the personal cost?

But this December had been the best month of his life. A January without Elfie and Walter seemed bleak indeed.

He opened the first envelope and started reading, pushing it aside with a snort at the demand for money. No wonder Elfie looked so miserable. The next half hour was no better and he could feel indignation rising at the depths people would go to in order to make an easy buck, when an exclamation from Elfie made him look up.

'Read this,' she said, handing him a lined sheet of notepaper. He quickly scanned the shaky lines.

*Dear Lord Thornham,*
*Thank you for taking in my Walter. Leaving him as I did was the hardest thing, but the local shelter had no room for him, I have no family locally and I was worried he'd end up in the pound when they took me to the hospice.*

*I'm sure I don't need to tell you how special he is. Since my Barbara died, I've found it hard to find the joy in life. We were never blessed with children and she was the one for making friends. And then my neighbours got a puppy they couldn't manage, and I found myself with a dog.*

*Maybe I was selfish, taking him in at my age, but he's brought me such joy. I hope he brings you as much. Please tell him I'm sorry and that I love him. I hope he still has the blanket and squirrel. They were always his favourites.*
*Thank you again.*
*Dennis Barnes*

Xander blinked, his chest full with sorrow at the short note. 'There is no demand for money.'

'No.' Elfie's eyes were bright with tears. 'All he wants is for Walter to have a good home.'

Turning over the envelope, Xander noticed an address sticker. 'Dennis is quite nearby… the hospice is just a few miles away.'

'There's no happy reunion for Walter; it's just us,' Elfie said softly. 'At least, it's just you, I suppose. Although I'll visit when I can.' Her voice broke. 'Xander. We have to take him to visit his old owner. He should say a proper goodbye.'

There were at least fifty unread emails in his inbox, half marked urgent, a pile of contracts and other correspondence on his desk. Tomorrow was Christmas Eve, which meant a move to Thornham Park, the festive season and all its calls on his time was in full swing. But there was something about the wonky lines on the tattered paper that touched him. The writer was alone in a hospice and Walter was his only family. Xander knew what it was like to feel alone in the world, and he knew Elfie did too. 'I'll order the car.'

Any doubts over their decision disappeared the minute a nurse ushered them into a cheerful but unmistakably medical room, hung with tinsel and other decorations, where an elderly man lay in bed, hooked up to tubes, his breathing laboured.

'Dennis talks about Walter a lot; he'll be so glad to see him,' she said quietly as she showed them in. The hospice, for all its comfortable, home-like air, still smelt of boiled food and antiseptic, just like the home where Xander's father had spent his last few months, and Xander inhaled shakily, memories of long days and nights spent at the side of the man he could never please, not even at the end, filling his mind. There had been no deathbed affection or confession of love, just demands for business updates and admonitions and orders. To keep the estate together and profitable, to marry soon and wisely and father an heir. To stop hiding behind his desk and to get out there. To be a Montague, to be worthy of the name. To not let them down. To be a man. He swallowed. Now he could never show his father he had what it took. That maybe he always had.

Walter whined softly, recalling Xander to the reason they were here, and Xander scooped him up, carrying him over to the hospital bed, Elfie at his side.

'Mr Barnes,' she said in a soft voice. 'Mr Barnes, I am Elfie and this is Xander. We've brought Walter to see you.'

Dennis's eyes fluttered open and he blinked uncertainly before recognition and hope flooded his face, tears welling in his eyes. 'Walter?' he asked as the dog whined again. 'Is that you, boy?'

Elfie set a chair by the bed and they placed Walter on it so that his old owner could reach him, laying a wrinkled hand on the dog's head. Walter whined again, pushing very gently against the hand as if he knew how careful he needed to be.

'I never thought I'd see you again. I knew it was wicked leaving him, but that shelter has such a good reputation. If anyone could find you the home you deserve...' His voice was as laboured as his breathing and he came to a painful-sounding stop.

'You did the right thing,' Elfie said, taking his hand with such natural sympathy Xander ached to see it. 'Walter is loved and cared for and happy. He's going to live in the country-side and have lots of space to play and Xander is going to make sure he's well looked after. We promise, don't we, Xander?'

'Yes, I promise.' But Xander was uneas-ily aware that the promise wasn't quite as it seemed. Walter would live at Thornham Park and would be well taken care of, but Elfie would be gone and Xander himself an oc-casional visitor. The dog had already been passed from home to home in his short life; he deserved stability, to be with someone who wanted him, not someone who was paid to take care of him.

Maybe he was over-identifying with the dog. But Xander could remember the first Christ-mas after he'd been sent to boarding school, arriving back at Thornham Park to find all his family away and no spare bedroom put aside for him. He'd been given a room at the manager's estate house until an au pair had finally shown up to take him back to London for the next few days. He'd heard the other boys talking excitedly about going home, about their families, their houses, their bedrooms, desperate to get back to those familiar places. Whereas Xander had loved the routine of school. To sleep in the same bed every night, to be cared for by the same people, to know what was expected of him.

Maybe he could keep Walter with him whenever he was in the UK after all. With his mother in France and the American hotels attracting a more transitory experience seeking clientele, he didn't need to spend as much time abroad as his father and grandfather had. And he had already determined to have a wing at Thornham Park or maybe the Dower House as a permanent home once he was married and had children, to ensure no child of his grew up with no sense of home. He could start now, carve out space for Walter and him.

He stole a glance at Elfie as she chatted softly to Dennis, telling him about the day she had first met Walter and known he was the one, making the elderly man laugh a wheezing chuckle as she recounted how the dog had performed tricks to get her attention, how he had adapted to hotel life and always seemed to know who to make eyes at for treats.

'All the hotel staff adore him,' she continued. 'But, most importantly, he's happy. I know he misses you; now I've met you I understand why he gets excited when we see men of your age. But he *is* happy. He has his favourite walk, his favourite corner of the sofa, has made friends with the most soft-hearted chefs and eats better than some of the guests. I hope that's of some comfort.'

'More comfort than you can know.'

Yes, maybe there was a way he could balance his nomadic life and keep Walter. It was a shame he couldn't do the same for Elfie. New Year was just over a week away. A week after that she would be packing and off on her next adventure. It was too soon. Far too soon.

It was a quiet journey back to the hotel, both of them lost in thought, while Walter was unusually subdued, lying with his head on Elfie's knee. She stroked his ears softly, heart aching for the dog and his owner. She'd promised to return next week and hoped Xander would continue to visit after she had left for as long as it was possible.

'Are you okay?' Xander asked and she nodded.

'Just thinking about Dennis. How hard it

must have been to make the choice to leave Walter the way he did, how he must have felt like he was abandoning him, even if his intentions were good. To be that alone in the world when the end comes, so alone that there's no one to visit or take care of your dog…' Her voice trailed off. She had always told herself that it was safest to be alone, that it meant never getting hurt, that you couldn't destroy what and who you loved, that you couldn't be left behind, but there was a downside to it too.

'But it sounds like he had a happy life. Did you see the pictures by his bed, of him and his wife? They were laughing in every single one, not forced smiles but real laughter. I never saw my parents laugh together like that.'

'Mine did. It was one of the things I missed most afterwards. The house was so quiet…' She looked out of the window and realised they were near the park. 'I think Walter should have a walk,' she said. 'Can we stop the car? I'll walk him back to the hotel.'

'Would you mind company?'

'Not at all, but I thought you had a lot to do?'

Xander grimaced. 'So much that another half an hour's skiving won't really make a difference.' He leaned forward to talk to the driver and less than a minute later the car glided to a stop, the driver jumping out to open Elfie's door and help Walter get out.

The afternoon was turning to dusk, the air bitterly cold with a sharp wind, and Elfie pulled her coat around her, shivering. Not that she needed to put up with this for much longer; in a couple of weeks she'd be in the Caribbean for a lucrative charter season and the chance to get some much-needed vitamin D. She waited for the usual feeling of pleasurable anticipation to ripple through her, but instead she felt numb—numb until Xander took her hand and then her whole body warmed up in one almighty whoosh of flame. It was embarrassing how much effect a touch separated by two layers of wool had on her, how instantly she responded to the lightest of caresses.

The lights of the Christmas fair flashed in front of them and by unspoken accord they turned down a quieter path, Walter stopping and sniffing every frosty leaf. 'I admit it. You did a good thing,' Xander said at last.

'Me?' Elfie was genuinely surprised.

'Choosing Walter.'

'I think he chose me, to be honest.' She paused, looking for the right words. 'I was unsure at first. You were so disinterested, not even coming along to choose him, and then

I realised that you weren't even intending to keep him, not properly. I nearly walked away.'

'Why didn't you?'

She screwed up her face in embarrassment. 'Money,' she admitted. 'I couldn't run the risk of being sacked before I was due to fly out to my next job, and I knew this job could do wonders for my profile. You wouldn't believe how many people take social media popularity into account when hiring seasonal staff. Not everyone, some of the super-rich will pay a lot more for privacy, but my dog nanny account was getting me some seriously lucrative offers.' She bent down and ruffled Walter's head. 'I'm no better than any of those scam artists, am I? Sorry, Walter.'

'You were willing to work for every penny. You've put Walter's comfort before yours every time—you never mentioned how much he hogs the bed or how loudly he snores.'

'I find his snores soothing. But, I have to admit, I found it uncomfortable lying to Dennis then. He thinks Walter is going to have a happy ever after with us and instead...'

'He is. He stays with me unless I have to travel, and he'll have one carer when I am away. You're right; it's not fair on him otherwise.'

Relief filled her, a weight she hadn't realised

she was carrying, a guilt she'd been ashamed to admit to lifting her. 'Really? Oh, I am so pleased.'

'He'll miss you, though. We both will.'

'And I'll miss you too, but this is really the best news. You two are made for each other.' She turned to him, laughing. 'And you thought you wanted some kind of noble hound!'

'I told you, I admit I was wrong. Walter was the right dog for the job, and you were exactly the right person. Are the right person.' His grip on her hand tightened, pulling her towards him, and she leaned in, enjoying the uniqueness of this public embrace—they were alone in the lane, but this was Hyde Park; they could be interrupted at any moment. But as Xander tilted her chin, staring at her with an oddly serious expression she couldn't interpret, she forgot where she was and how cold it was, lost in the darkness of his velvety brown eyes.

'Hey,' she half whispered, a little unnerved by the intensity she sensed in him. By the way she wanted to sink into him. She was consumed by him, by the need to touch him, kiss him. Impatient, she tugged his head down to hers, cursing her lack of height as she reached up and brushed his mouth with hers, then again, harder this time. She didn't want sweet, slow caresses; she wanted hard and demanding, the type that left her mouth swollen and her body reeling with desire. She felt him laugh gently against her mouth.

'There's no rush.'

What was he talking about? Of course there was a rush! Their time here was finite, and the clock was ticking. She was off on her next adventure and he needed to pick a suitable Baroness and settle down to his responsibilities. There could be no repeat of this time. So they had to make the most of every single second.

She nudged closer until she was pressed tight against him, exultant as he groaned and deepened, intensified the kiss. For a moment the world went away, the cold and noise receding as she lost herself in him, until something banged against her leg, causing her to stagger to the side, righting herself as an insistent head butted her again.

'I think it's Walter's dinner time,' she said, aware that she was a little breathless, that her head was spinning.

Xander's mouth curved into a smile so deliciously wolfish her toes curled and she might have actually moaned out loud. 'I was thinking it was time we moved somewhere warmer and more private anyway. Shall we?'

He offered her his arm in that peculiarly old-fashioned, gallant gesture of his and she took it with equal ceremony. 'I'm cold.' She gave an exaggerated shiver and summoned up her most limpidly innocent expression. 'I think I need a long hot shower. Care to join me?'

# CHAPTER NINE

ELFIE KNEW THE super-rich. She had nannied for families in the heart of New York's most exclusive areas, whose two-storey penthouses had the kind of iconic views most people only saw in film sets. She had been a maid in chalets the size of hotels, fitted with every luxury money could buy, and crewed on yachts worth the same as a small country's GDP. She wasn't easily impressed.

Or so she thought. But when the car swept up the long driveway leading to Thornham Park she found her mouth falling open in awe, audibly gasping as the graceful—and huge—house finally came into sight, lit up against the winter-dark sky. Built in a gorgeous honey-coloured stone and surrounded by green, flower-filled terraces even in winter, the house rose in tiers, the stonework as lavishly decorated as any wedding cake. It was surrounded by acres of parkland and woodland, the farms which had once fed the great house on the very outskirts of the land.

Dusk had fallen and lights were entwined in the trees nearest the house, creating a magical effect, the tall pine trees which signalled the end of the drive tastefully and seasonally decorated. 'It's beautiful,' she breathed as the car came to a stop and Xander escorted her up the grand stone steps leading to the imposing front door and into the great hall, which doubled as a comfortable sitting room and reception with a roaring fire in the gigantic mantelpiece. Like Thornham House, the decorations were lavish, with greenery on every surface and a huge Christmas tree dominating the hall, presents already laid out underneath.

Xander greeted the reception staff and a few guests who obviously knew him well as one porter collected their cases and another disappeared outdoors discreetly with Walter. Elfie hung back for a moment, unaccountably shy. No one questioned her place in London. She was one of them, a member of staff, and they all knew that her friendship with Xander was part of her job. If anyone suspected the truth about the turn their relationship had taken— and a hotel was a small community, after all—

she had heard no gossip. But she knew no one here and her status felt uncertain, neither guest nor staff nor family.

But she did have a job to do, she reminded herself, pulling out her camera and starting to document the festive scene. A place. For now, at least.

For a few moments she lost herself, as she loved to do, focusing on small details in order to bring the scene to life: a stocking hanging on the grand staircase, an exquisite crystal bauble, the heart of the fire. After a while she turned her focus onto people, on Xander talking to a regal-looking woman who seemed to be an old friend, the discreet waiters refilling glasses and offering canapés, the doorman standing to attention, as always trying to set them in their scene, looking for the story behind the pose.

There was something satisfying about seeing the world through a lens, being able to put a barrier between herself and the place and people she was photographing, letting her be a legitimate observer, aside from the action, just as she preferred it. She was only recalled to her surroundings when one of the receptionists offered her a glass of champagne and offered to show her to her room. Xander was still engrossed in conversation and, not wanting to appear needy or to look as if she expected more from him than their situation warranted, Elfie smiled her thanks, collecting Walter from the doorman as she followed the receptionist up the stairs, the dog butting at her heels.

'Here you are, Miss Townsend,' the receptionist said as she opened a heavy oak door. 'The Queen Victoria suite.'

'Please do call me Elfie. I am here to work, after all.' Elfie smiled her thanks as she stepped into the suite, stopping to gaze about herself in awe. 'Wow, this is really something.'

It really was. She'd loved the comfortable suite in London, but these rooms took her breath away. Richly decorated in red and gold, with high ceilings and huge old windows, it was easy to imagine herself back in time as she took in the elegant sitting room, her bedroom with its own seating area as well as bathroom and dressing room and the elegant little breakfast room which led out to its own private terrace. Her bags and Walter's bed were already in her room, her clothes unpacked and put away, her collection of practical layers even more incongruous than usual in the antique wardrobe, more accustomed to couture than hardwearing clothes.

Katya, the receptionist, gave her a quick tour, showing her all the very modern modifications hiding behind the antiques, from a state-of-the-art sound system to a cinema-sized screen. Elfie enjoyed playing with the gadgets, waiting until Katya left before exploring Xander's even more lavish room. After promising herself a long soak in his sunken double bath, she pulled her coat back on and stepped out onto the terrace to take in the view as she finished her champagne.

How things had changed in the last month. She'd been expecting to spend Christmas walking pampered pooches stuffed full of Christmas treats, before heading back to her dorm room. It wouldn't have been entirely joyless; she knew that a good Christmas dinner was always served to any working staff, and there were usually plenty of people in the hostel up for a transitory friendship she could have partied with. Instead, here she was in a room fit for a princess, waiting for the only lover she'd ever had who she couldn't get enough of.

Shouldn't she be getting bored by now? Finding the intimacy too confining? It was the chase she loved, those long looks and unspoken meanings. Possibilities and butterflies. Sometimes Elfie thought she would be happy staying in the flirtation stage for ever. But this time her feet weren't remotely itchy yet, the end looming, closer than she liked.

She looked round as she heard the door click and Walter left her to run, tail wagging enthusiastically, into the sitting room, only to return at Xander's heels.

'How long have you been standing out here? It's freezing.' He slipped an arm around her. The casual caress felt so normal, so comforting, and Elfie leaned in, seeking even closer contact.

'The view is stunning, though, even in the dark, the way the trees silhouette, thanks to the Christmas lights. No moon, though—look at the sky. It's so heavy. Do you think it will snow?'

'You want a white Christmas?'

'Always. This place is just gorgeous. I can't believe it's your family home.'

'I'm glad you approve. You don't mind sharing it with two hundred strangers?'

'It seems fair. A place this size is probably a bit much for one family to keep up nowadays.'

'It needs an army.' He nodded at her glass. 'Do you want a top-up before you get ready?'

'Sounds lovely.' She handed her glass to him and followed him as he took it into the sitting room, where a chilled bottle was waiting. He extracted the cork seamlessly and filled first her glass and then his own. She raised it in a toast and then paused as his last words sank in. 'Thank you. What did you mean, get ready?'

'For the ball.'

'Me?' She took a sip, confusion washing through her. 'Xander, you never said you wanted me to attend the ball. I assumed I'd be on Walter duty. We were planning room service and a Christmas film, weren't we, Walter? He was trying to convince me that *Die Hard* is a Christmas film, and I was trying to persuade him to give *Love Actually* a go.' Elfie knew she was chattering on, but she couldn't stop herself. She was here to look after the dog, not be Xander's date at the most prestigious night in the hotel's calendar.

The Thornham Park Christmas Eve Ball was legendary, its roots stretching far back into Georgian times, and the reason so many guests returned year after year for the festive season. The great and the good of the local area were also invited, along with Xander's extended family and old family friends—people with pedigrees as long as Xander's—who travelled into Buckinghamshire from London or their own home county homes for the event, just as their grandfathers and great-grandfathers had done. The kind of magazines who concentrated on the world of the aristocracy usually sent a reporter and a photographer to cover the evening, and minor royalty had been known to attend.

If she went to the ball as a guest, not as a member of staff, on Xander's arm, then they would be making the kind of public declaration they had been carefully avoiding, an acknowledgement that she wasn't just staff, and what was the point of arousing that kind of speculation? This thing between them might be the most intoxicating affair she had ever indulged in, but it had just over a week left to run. She turned to Xander, a determinedly light smile on her face. 'Is Walter coming too? He doesn't have a tux!'

'For a couple of photos, but then I've arranged for him to stay with one of the managers and his family for the night.' Xander's forehead creased, and she wanted to reach up and smooth the lines away. 'Don't you want to come?'

'Do I want to be part of the famous Thornham Park ball? Of course.' She was only partly lying. Although she would rather not court notice and gossip, part of her was intrigued by the idea of attending. After all, the ball was the epitome of glamour and for once she would be the one sipping the cocktails, not the one serving them. 'But Xander, you might have noticed that I have a limited and functional wardrobe. I'm not sure my trusty maxi dress and a pair of silver flip-flops will cut it.'

'Then it's lucky that you traditionally get your presents on Christmas Eve, isn't it?' His eyes were alight with laughter and her stomach twisted with a poignant desire. 'Go look in the wardrobe in my room.'

'What?' She set her glass down carefully and walked slowly into Xander's bedroom, aware that both he and Walter were at her heels, and opened the heavy wardrobe door, stepping back in surprise. 'Oh, my goodness! What is this?'

It was like setting foot in an alternate universe, walking into the wardrobe to find an up-market boutique. She could see at least eight styles of dress hung up, each in a couple of different sizes and colours. Propped on the open shelves were a variety of shoes and accessories. She whirled round to look at Xander, leaning against the wall with a proud grin on his face.

'Are you Prince Charming or the Fairy God-mother in this scenario? This is insane!'

'I didn't want to guess your style or taste and get it wrong. I have too many memories of my mother returning jewellery or clothes my father gave her to take such a risk. Anything you don't choose will go back to the store, but hopefully there will be something you like here.'

Elfie ran her gaze over the assorted dresses in rich shades of red and green, subtle ice blue and silver, and couldn't help a grin spreading over her face. 'I'm sure I can make do. How long have I got? I have some serious work to do.'

Normally Xander dreaded the annual Thornham Park Christmas Eve Ball. As host he needed to personally greet every single guest and dance with as many women as possible, favouring none. It gave him some kind of insight as to how it must have been in Georgian times, adhering to a rigid set of social customs. But tonight he was filled with an unexpected anticipation. Tonight he would have Elfie next to him, in his arms, and that knowledge turned a chore into a treat.

The truth was the last month had been the best in his life and that was all down to Elfie. Not just because of the mind-blowing sex, not just because he had opened up to her in a way he had never opened up before, but because she had blown open his solitary existence and introduced laughter and companionship. He knew his path, one of duty and tradition. He had never expected that sharing that path with someone else would make the journey a light-hearted stroll as opposed to a slog.

Now he knew that, how could he settle for the kind of loveless marriage he had assumed he was destined for? An understanding of the obligations a life with him entailed was important, but surely both he and any future wife deserved happiness and laughter too? It was hard to imagine sharing his life with anyone but Elfie, but she had her own destiny, and her dreams didn't involve an ancient title and the burden of a huge estate.

But tonight was Christmas Eve, and decisions about marriage lay somewhere in the future. Tonight for the first time he felt his duty less a burden and more of an honour with Elfie sparkling at his side. She was the queen of living for now, and he was going to take a leaf from her book and enjoy every moment they had left. He winked at her as they took their place in the formal receiving line by the huge double doors leading into the doorway and Elfie grinned back. 'You've got this,' she said. And she was right; he did.

The first half hour was always spent welcoming the guests into the ballroom. Most of the guests were known to him, and all wanted to express their condolences on the loss of his father, 'So sad, coming so soon after your grandfather's death', before turning their attention to Walter who, far from shying away from the noise and lights and crowds, was quite clearly in his element. It was astonishing how far his fame had spread; most guests had an inkling of his past and it turned out many were fellow dog owners, all with a tit-bit of advice. The receiving line, usually the most excruciating part of the evening, passed in a flash.

And next to him throughout it all was Elfie, camera in one hand, Walter's lead in the other. If she were to attend, she had told him, it needed to be in an official capacity as dog sitter and chronicler and, as a man whose every social occasion was also work, he had agreed. He knew that having a defined role could help someone face a room full of curious strangers. But although she might consider herself on duty she looked like the belle of the ball and he could hear several people asking who the woman with the extraordinary eyes was.

In the end she had chosen the simplest of the dresses he'd ordered, a soft dove grey, almost purple in some lights, blue in others, with a straight satin skirt and a soft georgette bodice. Sleeveless, it had a high modest neckline, dropping low at the back, revealing her delicate shoulder blades. She'd teamed it with teardrop earrings and a matching bracelet, her hair twisted into a low loose bun, tendrils framing her face. The colour accentuated the stormy grey of her eyes; the simplicity of the dress suited her petite frame. She was the most stunning woman in the room and seemingly neither knew it nor cared, happy for Walter to get hairs on her dress or walk on her hem. All Xander wanted to do was sweep her into his arms and dance the night away with her but he had hosting duties to fulfil.

Christmas Eve always followed the same pattern. A tantalisingly delicious array of canapés circulated the room along with champagne, festive cocktails and soft drinks, and a light buffet was laid out in the supper room for anyone who wanted anything more substantial. Transport was available to take anyone who wished into the village for Midnight Mass and when they returned mulled wine and mince pies were served, the traditional end of the ball.

A chamber orchestra provided accompaniment for traditional waltzes and foxtrots, alternating with a cover band who played a selection of tunes from the last fifty years. As a child Xander had found the evening stuffy and boring, as a young man a chore, but tonight he could see the charm in the festive ballroom with its holly and mistletoe themed decorations, in the gorgeous colours of the women's dresses and the elegance of the men's tuxedos. Children skidded across the dance floor and played hide and seek amongst the columns while the few teens in attendance posed for selfies.

The evening passed quickly. After anyone who wanted to had posed with Walter for a picture and he had been fed a carefully regulated amount of treats, one of the hotel managers took him back to the estate cottage where he lived with his family to settle the dog for the night. Xander had introduced Elfie to two of his closest friends, both of whom were here with their wives, and he was relieved to see that they took Elfie under their wing, ensuring she wasn't alone unless busy with her camera. Meanwhile he fulfilled his duty, moving around the ballroom and engaging each group in conversation, taking his father's place and asking some of the older ladies to dance when the orchestra played a waltz or foxtrot. Both his father and grandfather had been accomplished ballroom dancers and being asked by them had been considered something of a privilege. Xander had been brought up to know the difference between a waltz and a Viennese waltz and so he did his best to fill in, his reward the pleasure on the face of a woman who had been a close friend of his grandmother's when he led her onto the floor—and the approval in Elfie's eyes as she raised her camera to capture the opening dance.

It took a couple of hours to work his way around the room, but finally Xander found himself right where he wanted to be, next to Elfie, just as the orchestra started to play a slow waltz. He held out a hand. 'Dance with me?'

'I'm not sure I know how.' She took his hand, and he closed his fingers around hers. 'I've seen you out there tonight and you are good. How didn't I know you had moves?'

'I keep my talents close.'

'What else are you hiding from me?'

'Stick around a little longer and who knows

what you'll find out?' It was a light-hearted exchange, but Xander realised with a jolt how much he wanted the words to be true, for Elfie to stick around, to discover more about her as she did about him. For this not to be a month-long friendship, a two-week fling, but something more, something worth exploring.

Maybe there was a way. Could he ask her to stay here for longer, to see how they worked not as friends with benefits but as partners? Would she feel constrained and confined? And how could he ask her to give up her dreams for his duty?

There were no easy answers and so instead he pulled her close, leading her through a simple waltz. With one arm around her waist, her hand in his, feeling her hand splayed on his back it was easy to see how this old-fashioned dance had once been considered scandalous. He could feel every breath she took, see every expression that flitted across her face tilted up towards him, her lush mouth within kissing distance. How he wanted to whisk her behind a pillar and kiss her until all they could see were stars.

But the room was full of people who knew him and would be speculating about him; there were women here who he had dated, journalists and friends of his father. He couldn't, wouldn't expose Elfie to any gossip so instead he kept her close as they moved in perfect time.

'Are you sure you have never learned to waltz?' he asked, and she shook her head, her eyes dreamy as he twirled her through a turn.

'I always thought I had two left feet. You must be a very good teacher.'

'You make it easy.' And she did. She made everything easy, everything full of colour and light and possibility, and in a week she would be walking away and his life would be dull and dutiful once more.

Unless he figured out some way they could both get what they wanted and enticed her to stay.

'You always have that master of all you survey thing going on,' she said as the music stopped and he reluctantly stepped back, applauding with the rest of the couples as the orchestra bowed before making way for the band. 'But you have something else tonight. I can't quite work it out.'

Xander snagged two smoked salmon canapés from a passing waitress and handed one to Elfie. 'Debonair handsomeness and a devilish air?'

'Of course. Always. But it's something more.

You looked absolutely genuinely fine out there, especially when you were charming those women. I thought one might swoon when you danced with her! I'd promised myself to check in with you regularly, knowing how much you find these occasions a strain, but you looked okay. I know you cover it well, but either you're such an exceptional actor we need to get you on the stage right now or you are actually having a good time.'

'I was having a good time. I am.' He didn't know what surprised him most, the truth of the statement or the knowledge that Elfie had been keeping a watchful eye on him. That she knew him well enough to anticipate his fears and cared enough to look out for him. 'I'll be honest; I was dreading tonight, acting as the main and only host, knowing everyone is watching and comparing me to my father. Worried that I wouldn't know what to say and how to be and that everyone would be thinking I was arrogant. But you know what? I'm surprised by what a good evening I'm having. I hope you have been okay. I'm sorry I had to leave you so much.'

'Your friends have taken very good care of me. Are you allowed to dance twice with the same unmarried lady or will that cause a scandal? Because I may not know how to waltz but this song is a particular favourite of mine.'

'In that case, how can I resist?' He took her hand and headed back to the dance floor, now full of enthusiastic groups and couples dancing along to the famous disco tune. But as he joined in, watching Elfie laugh and twirl to the music, the question lingered in his mind. How could he resist her? More, how could he allow her to walk away when he wanted more, much more?

# CHAPTER TEN

SONG FOLDED INTO song and Elfie lost herself in the music. Xander's friends had joined them on the dance floor and so on the occasions he excused himself to speak to someone he had missed earlier, or to wave off an early departure, she stayed where she was, allowing her body to move to the beat and enjoy the sheer unadulterated pleasure of dancing. She might not have had lessons in ballroom dancing, but she enjoyed the chance to let go when she could and the excellent band and the festive atmosphere along with the unexpected connection with Xander's friends gave her the confidence to dance to every tune. Xander was such a cat that walked alone that she hadn't been sure what to expect from his close friends, but she had found herself drawn to them and their wives, all four unpretentious with a warm sense of humour.

The music finally slowed and the groups separated into swaying couples. Elfie retreated, glad of the break, aware that she was both thirsty and a little dishevelled. She helped herself to a glass of refreshing water garnished with mint and elderflower before searching for the restrooms, deciding against going upstairs to her suite.

The cloakrooms were as opulent as the rest of the hotel with a spacious seating area, a discreet screen shielding the entrance to the sinks and toilets. Several women around Elfie's age were lounging on the sofas, scrolling through their phones and gossiping. Elfie was aware of their stares as she walked through the room and headed to the sink, where she wanted to cool her flushed face before repairing her hair and make-up.

The water was deliciously refreshing as she patted her cheeks dry, searching through her bag for powder and lipstick and a comb to tackle her hair, which was beginning to collapse out of its bun after a few too many enthusiastic dances. Engrossed in her task, she tuned out the carrying voices from next door until she heard Xander mentioned.

'Xander looks hot tonight, don't you think?'

The answering voice had the kind of long

drawn-out drawl that provoked the same instinctive wince in Elfie as fingernails on a chalkboard. 'Xander always looks hot. That was never the issue. He has the looks, he has the money, he has all this...'

'So, what was the problem?'

'He was just no good at having fun. Even a weekend away was about scouting out the opposition. He never switches off. It's exhausting. And as for conversation? I swear he never heard a word I said.'

'He looked like he was having fun tonight,' a third voice said slyly, and a peal of laughter rang out. Elfie thought she heard someone ask, 'Who is that woman anyway?' and did her best to block out the voices. Eavesdroppers never heard any good of themselves; she'd learned that the hard way, sitting on the stairs and listening to her mother tell her stepfather that she was just going through a difficult phase. The old betrayal ran deep, and she felt her nails cut into her palms as she tried to stuff the hurt back into the past where it belonged, her ears ringing with memories. By the time her hearing had cleared and she had regained control, the laughter had died down.

'I heard a rumour he's ready to settle down,' the woman with the sly voice said.

'Of course he is; he's thirty now and he needs an heir. What about it, Cressie? Fancy being a baroness?'

'I'm considering it,' Cressie drawled. Elfie ran the name through her mind, through the research she had done on Xander. This must be Lady Cressida Wallington-Evans, a tall slender blonde who worked in banking. Brains, beauty and pedigree, she would be a perfect baroness, the kind of woman who would provide an heir and a spare whilst helping run the hotels and estate without breaking a sweat, no hair out of place and nails perfectly manicured as she did so.

'Well, if you don't want him let me know; I wouldn't mind owning all this. And I've always wondered what was under that forbidding exterior of his. I'd like to find out if still waters really do run deep.'

'If you do then let me know,' Cressie said with a laugh as annoying as her drawl. 'I never got anywhere, but luckily one doesn't need one's husband for all one's entertainment. I'd quite happily stay here while he travels around all the time. If I say yes.'

'If he asks you, you mean!'

'Darling, if I want him to then he'll ask me. That's not a worry.'

And with that they were gone, leaving Elfie leaning against the sink feeling a little like Cinderella watching the coach turn back into a pumpkin. She wasn't quite sure what she made of the conversation she'd inadvertently overheard but she did know three things. One, Lady Cressida Wallington-Evans would be looking elsewhere for a husband; Elfie would put a spoke in that particular young woman's wheel before she left if it was the last thing she did. No way was that woman going to have charge of Walter; she sounded like the kind of woman who made dogs sleep downstairs and would never share the last piece of cheese. Two, Xander should only marry someone he loved and respected and who loved and respected him, heir or no heir. Because he was worth more than his title and the estate he had inherited, worth more than the continuation of a family name, and he deserved someone who knew that. Someone who wanted the man, not the trappings.

And three, she had had a timely reminder that, fun as tonight had been, this wasn't her world, and this wasn't her life. She was getting too close to forgetting who she was, why she was here, getting in way too deep, behaving as if they really were a couple, as if this time didn't have an end date. Living in the moment was all very well but she was in danger of thinking the moment was reality.

She had to be careful, rein in her emotions, remember her mantra of moving on while it was still fun. Before she outstayed her welcome. Before she found herself outside looking in once again. Because she had a feeling that this time finding herself rejected would hurt more than it ever had before. And last time had been unbearable.

She took another look in the mirror, chin tilted defiantly, eyes flashing. She was a survivor. An independent woman. She had been on her own for the last decade and that was the way she liked it. A romantic fairy tale fling couldn't, wouldn't change that. No matter how much part of her wanted it to. The part of her that still believed in happy ever afters despite all the evidence to the contrary, the part of her that still yearned to be loved, wanted to be loved no matter the cost.

It was Elfie's job to protect that part of her, to keep the armour polished, to mend all chinks. She and Xander were about a bit of festive fun. She needed to remember that and walk away without a backwards glance, just like she always did.

* * *

It was late by the time the last car had driven
away, the last guest had gone to bed and Xander was free to return to their suite. He hadn't
seen Elfie for an hour or so; she had slipped
away pleading tiredness and he thought she
would probably be asleep. So it was a surprise
when he walked into the suite to find the lamps
on and Elfie curled up on the sofa staring into
the distance, a wistfulness in her eyes that
made his heart ache. He knew she found this
time of year hard.

'Hey,' he said softly, and she looked up
slowly, her smile not reaching her eyes.

'Are you done now?'

He shrugged off his suit jacket and undid his
bow tie in relief. It was ridiculous how constricting he found formal clothes, considering
how much time he spent in them. 'Until the
morning. This time of year is always intense.'

'Next year you should take a year off. Come
and find me on a beach. We can swim and eat
ice cream for Christmas dinner.'

'Sounds like heaven.' He felt a piercing ache
at the thought that he would never see her
bathed in sun, never watch her emerge from
the sea, hair wet and plastered back, bikini-
clad and glowing. He'd never really cared be-

fore, when a relationship neared its end, never wanted to take the moment and hold it tight, to escape time.

'My friends liked you.' He perched on the sofa arm and Elfie shifted so her head was in his lap, her hair spilling out. He took a tendril and wound it gently around his fingers.

'I liked them. Where did you meet them?'

'Prep school. Most people think it's barbaric to send kids away to school at seven, and it's not something I would do, but the truth is I loved school. Loved the security, the routine. I shared a room with Tim and Leo and although we were all so different we became close, like brothers, I suppose. The nearest thing I have, anyway. We all went on to the same senior school and our friendship endured.' He smoothed her hair out, selecting another tendril. 'My parents loved Tim; he was exactly the kind of sports mad daredevil they wished I was, and Leo was always throwing himself behind one cause or another; I guess politics was an inevitable career path for him.'

Her eyes were half closed. 'They're very fond of you. I get the feeling they worry about you. We all need people to look out for us. I'm glad you have them.'

His hands stilled. 'Has someone been telling tales out of school?'

She sat up, turning to face him, taking his hands in hers. 'Not at all. They were just talking about your university days and one of them mentioned that your teachers had tried to encourage you to choose maths. Apparently, you were a bit of a child prodigy.'

That was the problem with friends who had known him since he was small. Friends who'd always tried to invite him home for holidays because they knew he might be heading back to an anonymous hotel room and another temporary nanny. Friends who knew how much he relished the rituals of tradition, of knowing where things were, and hated change. Friends who'd watched him attend every pure maths lecture he could, even as he'd pushed himself to engage with the degree he had chosen.

'I don't believe in looking back, in regrets. Besides, I never had that genius spark needed to pursue maths,' he said, and it was true. He just would have liked the journey.

Her eyelids flickered but she didn't speak and Xander wondered just what had been said during his absence. His friends had very determined views, not just on his career path but on the relationships he pursued and his plans for his future marriage as well.

'You looked very beautiful tonight. The most beautiful woman there.'

The pensive, almost fragile look left her eyes as she smiled and cupped his face with her hands. 'You don't need to flatter me. I already intended you would get lucky tonight.'

He raised his eyebrows. 'Did you? Then lucky is indeed the word.'

Shifting forward, Elfie leaned in and kissed him. It was a sweet, almost poignant kiss, her lips soft on his, her hands still on his cheeks. He pulled her closer, one hand tangling in her hair, the other skimming over the exposed skin of her back.

'I'm glad you chose this dress,' he murmured against her mouth and felt her smile.

'You like?'

He traced her shoulder blade and felt her quiver. 'Very much.'

Now it was Xander's turn to kiss her, deeper, passionate, but still with a hint of wistfulness, as if they were both keeping an eye on the clock and watching their time together run out. Her arms wound around his neck, clutching his nape, pressing so close he could feel her imprinted on him. Slowly, still kissing her, he stood up, bringing her with him.

'Lovely as this sofa is, I am ready to retire for the night. You?'

'I think I could be persuaded.' She took his hand, but Xander resisted as she tugged him towards the bedroom door.

'Aren't you forgetting something?'

She stopped, hand still in his, biting her bottom lip in query. 'I thought Walter was staying away tonight?'

'It's Christmas Eve,' he reminded her and looked deliberately down at her feet, covered by the hem of her dress. 'Shouldn't you be leaving shoes out?'

'I'm a little old for that.' She attempted a smile, but her mouth wobbled and he knew she was thinking about the last Christmas she'd attempted to do so. 'I'm sure Father Christmas is busy with the children tonight.'

'It doesn't hurt to try.'

'I guess not.' She slipped off first one and then the other of the high heeled silver shoes she'd chosen to wear with the dress. 'I can't believe I haven't got blisters; I never wear heels. But then I've never been able to afford this brand before.' Gathering up her shoes, Elfie placed them by the Christmas tree that dominated the far corner of the room and then grinned at Xander. 'Go on; you too.'

'Me?'

'I can't imagine Father Christmas coming here just for me.' Her tone was teasing and Xander laughed as he removed his shoes and placed them next to hers before turning to look at her, mouth swollen, hair tumbling over her shoulders, dimly aware that he had laughed more in the last month than the last decade. But as her eyes darkened with desire, her chest moving with each breath, and his own body heated in response, amusement fled, replaced with a primal need. *Mine* every sinew, every beat of his heart, every nerve, every drop of blood claimed. *Mine*.

He stepped towards her and stood looking at her for one eternal second while the blood thundered around his body before scooping her up, his mouth fastening on hers as he carried her through the sitting room and into the lamplit bedroom.

It was like going back in time, living out her Mr Darcy fantasies as she was ruthlessly swept off her feet and thoroughly kissed before being deposited onto a four-poster bed older than most people's houses. Excitement lit every nerve as Elfie scooted up the blessedly modern mattress to support herself against the pillows and watch as Xander undid every button on his shirt before shrugging it off, moving with that same deliberate haste onto his belt, until his trousers slid to the floor, stepping out of them with careless grace. The breath whooshed from her body as Elfie took him in, greedily exploring every inch of him with her eyes, capturing him in detail so that in a week, a month, a year she would be able to recall just how the lamplight moved over honed muscle, how the shadows emphasised the sharpness of his cheekbones, the darkness of his eyes. He was magnificent and he was hers.

The silk of the dress felt almost unbearable on her heated skin, but when she went to unzip it Xander held up a hand. 'Wait. I want to undress you.'

Her stomach jolted at the words, her breasts heavy and yearning for his touch as she mutely nodded. But he didn't join her, not yet. Instead he stood at the bottom of the bed, clad only in his boxer shorts, examining every inch of her in turn. She could physically feel the journey of his gaze sliding up her legs, along her stomach, moving slowly over the curve of her breast. How could he turn her on so much without even touching her? Finally, he nodded in satisfaction, sitting on the side of the bed, only to torture her further by retracing the path of his gaze with his fingers, gliding along the satin on a torturous, almost unendurable journey. She shifted restlessly and his hands stilled, a wolfish smile playing on his mouth. 'Patience.'

Eyes, fingers and then mouth following that same heated trail, the sensation of touch on satin shooting through her until at last she felt the zip give way as Xander eased it down her trembling body, before repeating the same slow undressing with her underwear, the same slow intense exploration of her body, this time skin to skin. By the time he came to her she was mindless with need, reaching for him, needing his body heavy on hers, his mouth crushing hers, to be enveloped by him, gasping at the rightness of him, of them together. She'd been expecting lovemaking as dark and intense as the foreplay, but it was unexpectedly tender and sweet, their gazes locked together, their bodies as one.

It had been so long since she'd felt so wanted, so cherished, so needed. How could she just walk away in a week with a breezy goodbye as if this hadn't been the most meaningful, intimate experience in her life? But Xander had plans that didn't involve her—and she had to keep her heart safe. Difficult as leaving would be, staying would be infinitely more dangerous. So she needed to hold onto this moment, this night, this week and let its warmth sustain her over the months ahead. Memories were all she could allow herself; she needed to make sure they were perfect.

## CHAPTER ELEVEN

It took Elfie a couple of moments to name the tingle of anticipation in the air when she woke up. Christmas! She turned, burying herself into Xander's side, smiling to herself at the ludicrousness of a grown woman feeling this excited on Christmas morning. But then she hadn't shared Christmas with anyone for a very long time.

She allowed herself a few minutes to enjoy the feeling. Xander was still asleep, warm and solid to her touch and all hers. She wrapped herself around him, her breathing slowing to match his, drifting back into a contented doze, when she felt him shift, pulling her even closer.

'Good morning—or should I say Merry Christmas?'

'Merry Christmas to you too.' She reached up to press a kiss on his cheek. 'Do you think Father Christmas has visited?' She couldn't quite hide her smug smile. It had taken some stealth to sneak out of bed, retrieve his gifts and put them under the tree while he slept, but she had managed it.

Xander checked his watch. 'Plenty of time before breakfast. Shall we go and see?'

He rolled out of bed and she watched him with shameless approval as he crossed the bedroom naked, only to reappear from the bathroom in a hotel robe, another one slung over his arm which he handed to Elfie. She put it on, fastening the cord around her waist, and ran her fingers through her hair before following Xander into the suite's sitting room, only to pause and gasp at the door.

While they had slept some elf had sneaked in and transformed the room. The tree was lit up, an enticing heap of presents set beneath it; more lights were strung across the mantelpiece. The small table in the corner had been laid, a pot of steaming coffee, jugs of fruit juice and a plate of cinnamon rolls placed there. Walter lay on his bed, thumping his tail, stretching to his feet as she walked in. 'How did you get here?' she asked him as he butted her hand in greeting.

'Christmas magic,' Xander said. 'Coffee?'

'Please.' She took the cup he proffered and

wandered over to the sofa and sat down, Walter jumping up to curl up beside her. 'I can't believe someone brought us breakfast and Walter and I didn't even hear.'

'I told you, Christmas magic. Have you checked your shoes yet?'

'Not yet; have you?'

They stayed still for a moment, smiling at each other, and Elfie wanted to take this second and freeze it, this feeling of affection and happiness, silly giddiness and anticipation before the present-opening began and Christmas started. She committed every detail to memory, the aromatic coffee scent mixed with pine and cinnamon, Xander with his morning stubble shadowing his chin and sleep-tousled hair, Walter's tail wagging furiously, the festive lights, the feeling of complete contentment. She didn't need presents; she just needed this.

'Okay,' she said at last, taking her coffee over to the tree. 'Let's take a look. Walter, there are several here with your name on; I wonder what they could be? Hey, Xander, looks like you've been a good boy; your shoes are nice and full.' She slid them towards him and he took them.

'How about you? Have you been a good girl?'

'Looks like Father Christmas thinks so.'

'He's not the only one.' Their eyes met, the atmosphere charged, before Walter jumped off the sofa, breaking the tension and, laughing, Elfie investigated the content of her shoes. Chocolate, some expensive-looking perfume, a pretty pair of silver earrings. She put the earrings on, watching Xander open his own gifts, also chocolate, a book on how to teach your dog tricks, some new gloves—she'd noticed he was always losing his—and some handmade soaps, small bottles of artisan liqueur and fudge she had bought at the craft fair held alongside the dog show.

Most of the presents under the tree were for Walter; not only had both Elfie and Xander bought him gifts but so, it seemed, had half the staff and by the time they'd finished helping him unwrap them he had quite the pile of toys and balls, treats and chews and a couple of smart coats and jumpers. Elfie took several photographs, most for his accounts, but one to send to Dennis so he could see how Walter was being spoiled and loved.

There had also been a few presents for Xander. A shirt from his mother, expensive malt whisky from one of his friends, a book from another. Usually, he explained, he would open them after Christmas dinner, downstairs with the guests, but this time he had wanted to enjoy a private Christmas for once. Elfie, on the other hand, wasn't expecting anything. She hadn't given her mother an address; normally money was deposited in her account on birthdays and Christmas, and she didn't have friends she exchanged gifts with. So she was more than a little surprised when Xander handed her a large brightly wrapped gift.

'For me?' She read the tag. 'Oh, Walter, you shouldn't have!' Once she would have torn the paper off, but she wanted to savour the moment, carefully peeling back the tape, teasing open the paper to reveal a huge rucksack from a brand she had always coveted but never been able to justify buying. 'Wow! Thank you, Walter.' She kissed the top of his head and then leaned over to kiss Xander as well. 'You have been generous with his pocket money.'

'He noticed that your bags were looking a little battered. Someone who is always on the move needs the right equipment.'

'He is very wise.'

There were just two gifts left now and, feeling more than a little nervous, Elfie picked up a flat package and handed it to Xander, her cheeks heating as he read the tag.

'To Xander, love Elfie and Walter.' She was embarrassed to think how long it had taken her to write the brief message, her pen hovering over the word love for what felt like hours.

'You didn't need to get me anything,' he said as he opened it and she shrugged.

'We wanted to, didn't we, Walter?'

She watched anxiously as he slid the picture out of its wrapping, his forehead crinkling as he looked at it. It was a simple pen and ink drawing of a scruffy dog she'd had framed, the initials AT in the corner, dated twenty years earlier.

'It's one of my dad's,' she explained. 'He often drew simple pictures like this to amuse me, and I realised how much this one looked like Walter.'

'It really does,' he said slowly. 'Of course, your father was Albert Townsend. Why didn't I make the connection? Elfie, this is way too valuable, both in sentimental and actual value. I can't accept this.'

'You know my dad's work?'

He nodded. 'Figgy worked at an art gallery; they had a display of your father's pictures while we were dating, and I went to the opening party. I was absolutely blown away by his use of colour and line. I promised myself I'd treat myself to one of his paintings one day.'

Elfie swallowed. 'My dad would have been so happy to hear that; I wish you could have met him. And of course you should keep it; he did me a lot of these little scribbles, mostly of animals, and I have them all safely stored with some of my childhood belongings. I'll never sell them. They weren't meant to be sold, they were just for me, but this one belongs to you.'

'You're sure?'

She nodded.

'Then I am honoured to accept it.' He leaned over to kiss her. 'Thank you. And this is for you.' He handed her the last present, labelled simply *For Elfie. X* in Xander's distinctive handwriting.

'But you gave me my gift last night.'

'That was to celebrate French Christmas; this one is for the English Christmas.'

She glanced at him uncertainly as she took the present and began to open it, her heart beating fast. The paper fell away to reveal an antique powder compact, delicately painted with a picture of a ballerina. She pressed the catch and as the lid sprung up a tune started to play. 'The Dance of the Sugar Plum Fairy,' she said in surprise. 'Oh, this is beautiful. I've never seen anything so exquisite.'

'It was my great-grandmother's. It seemed fitting to pass it onto you, considering the tune. Apparently, these musical compacts were quite the thing in the nineteen-forties. Do you like it?'

'I love it…it's absolutely perfect. Thank you.' She leaned in to kiss him, her heart hammering. These gifts weren't generic presents, chosen for passing ships, they were meaningful and personal for the giver as well as the receiver. And what that meant was more than she could process.

The rest of the day was mercifully busy, allowing her little time to dwell on the intimacy of the gifts. The hotel served a festive breakfast to the guests, followed by a series of activities ranging from walks to board games in the library, leading up to Christmas dinner itself. After dinner more gifts were exchanged and it was touching to see how many people clearly returned year after year, even buying presents for other guests. Xander and Walter both received plenty and the hotel, on Xander's behalf, had presents for every guest, handing out hampers full of homemade delicacies and blankets made from the Glen Thorne tartan.

But, for all the festivity and generosity, the care of the staff and the good humour of the guests, the day seemed to lack something and it wasn't until she took a photo of the whole group that Elfie realised what seemed strange—there were no children this year and, as no one commented on it, it clearly wasn't unusual. Elfie's heart ached to think of Xander spending so many childhood Christmases alone amongst strangers and adults.

For all his private fears of not living up to the family tradition, Xander was the consummate host, making sure no guest was excluded, as if this really were the private house party the hotel modelled itself on. It wasn't until presents had been exchanged, a vigorous game of charades concluded and guests had drifted off to read or nap that Elfie had him to herself once more.

'Let's take Walter for a walk,' she suggested. 'I could do with the exercise if I am going to have any chance of tackling the supper buffet.'

'Sounds like a plan.' He looked out of the window at the low heavy sky. 'Better wrap up warm; it looks like snow to me. You might get a white Christmas after all.'

Elfie dressed Walter in one of his new coats,

snapping and posting a picture as she did so, then met Xander at the back door. He was wearing his new gloves and held up his hands to her with a grin. 'Very cosy. Thank you.'

'Try not to lose them,' she said, and he shook his head.

'These came from you. I'll guard them well.' His tone was teasing but his expression was intense and the same heaviness that had hit her that morning pressed down on her. This was supposed to be fun, not serious. Somewhere along the way she'd taken her eyes off the road and things had accelerated without her even noticing. But it wasn't too late. She just needed to step back. Step back and head off like she always did.

And tell herself this time was no different.

But the conversation she'd overheard the night before was still churning through her brain. She couldn't walk away and leave Xander thinking he deserved a loveless sensible marriage when he deserved all the happiness in the world. She knew it; she just needed to make sure he did too. And then she could leave, her conscience clear.

By the time she reached the Caribbean this would all just be another adventure. She was almost sure of it.

\* \* \*

Elfie was unusually quiet as they left the hotel, gripping Xander's hand so tightly he could feel the pressure through their gloves. It was dark now, but fairy lights lit a path through the gardens and they followed it. There were no stars tonight, the clouds full and almost luminous. As they reached the rose garden the first snowflakes began to fall, dancing in the slight breeze. Elfie lifted her face up to the sky, eyes half closed.

'Making a wish?' Xander asked and she nodded.

'First snow of the season.'

He wanted to ask what she was wishing for, but something held him back. The cord that bound them felt so gossamer-thin, and although that was what they had both signed up for he was all too aware of its fragility, that he wanted to strengthen it, reinforce it, bind them together.

'Can I ask you to do something for me?' Elfie said abruptly and, surprised, he stopped, her hand still in his.

'Anything.'

'Promise me not to rush into marriage. Don't marry the kind of woman who you wouldn't trust to take good care of Walter if you weren't there.'

'The kind of woman who *what*?' Xander stared at Elfie in confusion.

She bit her lip, eyes lowered. 'I just think it will be a mistake if you choose someone to marry because of her family credentials or her CV. Don't pick someone who sees only the title and the estates and the money. Marry someone who sees you, Xander. Who wants to marry the man, not the Baron.'

Gently he reached out and touched her cheek and Elfie leaned into the caress. 'Hey, what brought this on?'

'I know you think that a quasi-arranged practical marriage is the sensible thing to do, but it isn't. It'll just drive you inside yourself and you deserve so much more than that. Don't marry someone who doesn't want *you*, Xander Montague, as opposed to Baron Thornham. Who you don't actually want and respect and love. Don't marry for heirs or because it's expected. So the title goes to a distant cousin? Does it really matter? Do you think Henry VIII's search for an heir was worth the lives of all those women, the disruption to the country—and in the end his great-nephew got the throne anyway and then his line died out. It's all meaningless when all is said and done.'

'I've never really thought of myself as Henry VIII before and I wasn't planning on executing my future wife if no heir appeared but...'

'I know! I just mean you can marry someone because she has the right name and credentials and be unhappy, but it won't necessarily give you the outcome you want. So why not be happy and see where it takes you?'

Her eyes, dark and intense, fixed on him as if she was willing her words into him. Words not dissimilar to his own thoughts over the last few weeks. Thoughts that had only started since he'd met her.

His world had rules for men like him: marry someone with the same background and ensure discretion if one looked for passion elsewhere. Xander had spent his whole life in that world and never met anyone he had wanted to invite in, to bare his soul to, to grow old with. The only woman to ever touch him in that way was Elfie.

But now he knew what it was like to hunger, to want, to need, to feel, to burn. Now he knew what happiness felt like. So how could he go back to merely existing? The truth was that confiding in Elfie didn't feel like weakness but like sanctuary and in return she had confided in him and he had taken her burdens willingly and gladly. How could he swap what they had for a loveless arrangement?

Loveless… It wasn't that he *loved* Elfie exactly; how could he? It was still so early, and he wasn't sure that he even knew what love was. But he liked her, desired her, wanted her to be happy. Surely that was close?

The snow had intensified, now falling thick and heavy, carpeting the ground in soft white, and Xander realised how cold it had become. Walter pressed close to his legs. 'Let's walk before we both get turned into icicles,' he said, tugging her hand. 'You're right. I've been thinking about my future too.'

'Well, that's good.'

'Elfie, I was raised to put duty first, to think that choosing any path for personal reasons was selfish, and I've always lived that way, not even knowing that something essential was missing as a result. But then I met you and everything changed. You're right. I do deserve more. We both do.'

He felt her stiffen, retreat. 'This isn't about me.'

'No? Shouldn't it be?' Every doubt, every

question he'd had about their next steps faded away. They were good together, really good. How could they turn away from something so rare, so special? 'You said yourself that I should be with someone who sees me, not the title. You do, Elfie, you see me.'

'Xander, what are you saying?'

'I'm saying stay. Don't go to the Caribbean. Stay with me. Let's see where this goes. We made the rules, Elfie; we can change them. We're good together. Let's not throw this away.'

Elfie dropped Xander's hand and backed away. 'No,' she said numbly. How could she have got it so wrong? 'I didn't mean me.'

'Why not?'

'Because I'm not the settling-down type. I don't want marriage and babies and all that.'

'I'm not talking about marriage, Elfie, at least not yet.' The excitement in Xander's face had faded, to be replaced by confusion, and it hurt her to realise she had caused it. 'And I know you want to fulfil your father's dream. But there's no reason you need to be alone to do that. Or that you can't do that from here.'

'It's not about the retreat. At least it's not just that. It's just this, us, right now, is perfect,

Xander. How we are is perfect. I don't want to ruin that.' Although she had an awful feeling it was too late to worry about ruining anything; the damage had been done. Why had she said anything? Why hadn't she saved her advice for the last day they were together?

'How will seeing where we go ruin what we have? Sure, we might not work out…but, Elfie, we might…we really might.'

'We won't!' She didn't mean to speak so loudly and heard the echoes of the words reverberate throughout the night. Lowering her voice, she half whispered, 'We won't. I'm sorry, Xander.'

The look of shock on his face cut her straight through to her heart. 'No, I'm the one who should apologise. I misread the situation, got carried away. Forget I said anything.' The snow was falling faster and faster, blanketing the ground, the trees, and she wished she could blanket her heart, her feelings, with the same numbing cold.

'It's not you.' Part of Elfie wanted to stay quiet, to shut the conversation down, but she couldn't let Xander think any part of her refusal was to do with him. Because it really wasn't. The way he had made her feel over the last few weeks, the way he took her seriously and yet made her feel like the most desirable woman alive. It was like magic, like living in a movie. Of course she was tempted to stay for a little longer. But it was because she was beginning to care so much for him that she had to make sure she wouldn't be tempted to push her luck any further.

Some men would shrug the rejection off, move onto the next woman in a matter of weeks, but Xander might see this as proof that he had been right to pursue his dutiful idea of a suitable marriage and she didn't want that for him. She wanted him to have it all, happiness and love and a house filled full of children with his eyes and puppies and kittens, like some kind of fifties bucolic fantasy. Just because she couldn't figure in that fantasy didn't mean he didn't deserve it.

'It's not you, Xander, it's all me.'

'Elfie…' He rubbed his gloved hand over his forehead. 'Honestly. You don't need to say anything, explain anything. Let's move on. I'm getting cold; shall we head back in for the buffet?'

She'd never felt less like eating in her life as he started back to the house, Walter looking back at her as she stood irresolute before breaking into a jog over the soft snow to catch up with him.

'Xander, I drive people away. That's what I do. I don't mean to, but it happens anyway, and I don't want that for you, for us. I want to remember us like we were this morning, not the moment you leave me.'

'So you'll leave me instead?'

'It's safer that way. I promise. For both of us.'

He stopped then and took hold of her shoulders. 'Who hurt you, Elfie? Who made you feel this way? I know your relationship with your mother is complicated, but…'

'Complicated? I wish. It's broken, Xander, and it's all my fault.'

'Elfie,' he said gently. 'Whatever happened, you were a child. No one can hold you responsible for anything. You certainly shouldn't allow it to dictate your whole life. I want you to stay, I want to see if this is just a passing attraction or something stronger. If you don't want to stay, if you know in your heart you don't have the right kind of feelings for me then that's fine. It has to be. But if you are walking away because you're scared or because of something that happened a long time ago then you are doing both of us a huge disservice.'

How she wanted to believe him, to take hold of his words and let them into her soul, but she had spent too many years hardening herself against everyone and everything to weaken now.

'I killed my father,' she said, holding his gaze. 'I killed my father and broke my mother's heart. Now do you see why you're better off without me, why I should always be alone?'

Elfie wasn't sure what she was expecting Xander to say, but she knew what she would see. Dawning disgust, revulsion, for him to step away. But, instead, he drew her closer, his eyes warm with a sympathy she knew she didn't deserve.

'You were twelve when your father died. He got run over. How could that be your fault?'

'Because he wouldn't have been out if it weren't for me,' she burst out, twisting out of his arms and walking as fast as she could through the swirling snow towards the hotel.

'Elfie, that doesn't make the accident your fault.'

She'd heard those words before, and she hadn't believed them then either. 'Who else was to blame? It was absolutely torrential rain, but he preferred to be outside rather than with me. I drove him out because I was bored and difficult.' The words were coming fast now, tumbling out as Xander grabbed her hand.

'Slow down, Elfie. It's okay.'

'It's not okay. It will never be okay.' She took a deep breath, glad of the numbing cold. 'His picture wasn't working but because of the weather he had to paint inside. I knew he needed space and quiet, but I'd been promised a trip out and I was grumpy, kept needling at him to play. I wouldn't leave him alone, no matter how many times he told me to, until he grabbed a coat and left because walking in the torrential rain was better than being inside with me. If I had just shut up, if I had just stepped away, then he wouldn't have been on that bend in that weather and he would be here now. Mum wouldn't have been left a widow and found herself a new family that didn't include me. I deserved it, though; I deserve to be alone.'

'That's the most ridiculous thing I have ever heard.'

Shocked, she stopped and turned to face him. *'What?'*

'Your father's death was an accident, a terrible, tragic, life-changing accident. And of course you can't help but wish you had done things differently, could go back and stop him, but that doesn't make any of it your fault. I'm sure your mother would say the same.'

But Elfie shook her head. 'I didn't want her to marry James. I begged her not to, told him I would never live in his house, and she was so angry. "Haven't you done enough?" she said. "Must you ruin everything?"' She stopped, horrified at the words, at the truths she had kept buried for so long. 'And she was right. I do ruin everything eventually, and I don't want to ruin us. I want to look back at these weeks and remember how happy we were. So can we go back and pretend all this never happened?' But, even as she said the words, she realised their futility. You could never go back; she knew that all too well.

Why had she spoken up? Why now? Because she was incapable of not self-sabotaging. She couldn't even get to the end of a fling without driving the other person away. Elfie blinked back hot, painful tears. She didn't cry, didn't regret, didn't look back.

'Let's talk about this inside.'

'No, I've already said too much; let's not talk about this again. But just because I'm not the right woman for you, Xander, doesn't mean that there isn't someone out there who is. Don't settle because we didn't work out, or because you think you should. I really want you to be happy.'

'But you can't want that for yourself?'

'I've learned not to,' she said so quietly she wasn't sure he'd heard her. But the words were true for all that. Fleeting happiness was all she deserved, and she knew not to hope for more. It was so much safer that way.

# CHAPTER TWELVE

IT WAS EARLY, still dark out, when Elfie awoke to find herself alone. Xander had obviously decided to take Walter out on a morning walk without her. She couldn't blame him because, although they had done their best to carry on as normal, their conversation in the snow and the secrets revealed had remained hanging over them, an almost tangible dark cloud. They'd somehow managed to put on a front during supper and the after-dinner games, as if they were the same people who had gone out on the walk, before returning to their suite to make love with an intensity she had never experienced before. But they weren't the same people. The innocence and fun had left their relationship.

She rolled over, pressing her hands over her face, wishing yet again that she had stayed quiet, that she could turn back the clock, could have stayed laughing, fun Elfie and not showed

Xander the darkness and bitterness within. But the damage was done and one thing was clear; she couldn't spend another week pretending nothing had changed. Elfie didn't know what would be worse, knowing that Xander still hoped she'd stay or knowing he'd changed his mind. Either way, staying wasn't an option.

She'd learned a long time ago to numb her emotions, but it took everything she had to stay focused as she swiftly packed. She hesitated for a while about using the new rucksack she'd been given but in the end she decided that leaving it would look petty, although she did reluctantly opt not to take the grey dress and shoes. There wasn't much use for them in a transient worker's life. She lingered for a long time over the compact, but in the end she couldn't bear to leave what it meant behind—the knowledge that someone had seen her, heard her, thought about her. Finally, she was done. She looked around at Walter's bed and toys, at Xander's possessions, at the picture she had given him and swallowed. Onto the next adventure, just a little earlier than planned.

She'd called a taxi before commencing packing and an alert told her it was here. Grabbing her bags, Elfie took a last longing look around. She would see such luxury again and soon, but she'd be on the other side of the metaphorical baize door, unpacking the bags, serving the meals, bringing the drinks. That was fine; she'd never been afraid of hard work. Hard emotions, however; they were another thing entirely. Which was why she was being such a coward and leaving without saying goodbye. She swallowed, trying not to think about Walter, already separated from one beloved caregiver. He had Xander; they would be fine. But what would they think when they returned and she wasn't here? She hesitated, irresolute, and it wasn't Walter's soulful eyes she was picturing, it was Xander's, full of hurt she would be responsible for.

Maybe he wouldn't be hurt, maybe he would be angry—or relieved that she had made parting so painless. Besides, it wasn't as if she had chosen to sneak away; she had no idea when Xander would return and every second she delayed was another tick on the taxi meter.

However, it wasn't until she was in the taxi that it dawned on Elfie that she didn't actually have anywhere to go. Her flight wasn't for a week, she'd given up her room at the hostel and as it was Boxing Day all transport was shut down and most hotels would be both expensive and booked up. She hadn't really thought out her departure. But then she hadn't thought any of this out very well.

'Whereabouts in London?' the taxi driver asked, and Elfie swallowed painfully. There was only one possible destination.

'Actually, I've changed my mind. Can we go to Surrey instead?'

She gave the taxi driver the address and then pulled out her phone, trying to think of anything to say to Xander that might make her actions look a little less pathetic. The right words wouldn't come, probably because there was nothing she could say. Finally, she simply texted.

I'm sorry. I truly believe this is for the best—and so do you now, probably. I really hope you find someone who makes you really happy. Love to Walter. X

And then she switched her phone off and sat back, eyes closed, wishing she could sleep the next week, next few months away. If her actions yesterday hadn't destroyed any illusions Xander had held about her then her decision to run away this morning would definitely have done so. Self-protection or self-sabotage? Elfie wasn't sure she even knew the difference any more. All she did know was that she would keep on working, saving, dreaming of a place she could call home and keep on protecting herself. And if that meant feeling so unbearably lonely she could barely face the next minute let alone the next hour then that was how it would be.

It seemed both no time at all and yet an eternity until the taxi drew up outside a large nineteen-thirties detached home on a quiet tree-lined road of similar houses. Elfie paid, turning down the driver's offer to carry her bags to the door, only belatedly realising that she was turning up without gifts. She had sent one, of course, like she did every year, a hamper for everyone, easy to order and hard to get wrong. But she should still have brought something for her siblings to open. Not that she had the faintest idea what to get for a twelve-year-old boy and ten-year-old girl she had barely spent any time with.

Swinging the rucksack onto her back, she picked up the other bag and started along the curved driveway. How she had hated this house when they'd moved here, with its ivy-covered red brick, but she had to admit it looked festive with the wreath on the front door and the lights entwined in the trees. She could see the

Christmas tree in the bay window and her chest tightened as she recognised one of the baubles as one from her childhood. She'd always thought her past had been subsumed into her mother's new family. Had she misremembered, too caught up in her pain and anger to see where there was partnership rather than a takeover?

Elfie stood by the front door, irresolute, for a long, long minute, trying to think of the right things to say, before she finally pressed the chiming doorbell. She heard footsteps thudding, a high-pitched voice yelling that they would get it and then the door was flung open and she found herself face to face with her half-brother.

'You're as tall as me,' she said stupidly, trying to think when she had last seen him. 'Hi, Polly,' she added to the smaller girl who had appeared at his side.

'Mum! Mummy! Guess what, Elfie's here! It's Elfie!'

'Who is it, Oliver? Polly, step away from the door and let me through.' Elfie's mother bustled up to the front door and stopped, her hand over her mouth. 'Oh, Elfie,' she said, her face crumpling. 'You came home for Christmas after all.'

\* \* \*

'I forgot that you always go out on Boxing Day; I'm sorry to have ruined your plans.' Elfie felt more than a little awkward as she walked along the snow-covered river path alongside her mother. Despite that awkwardness, she was relieved that her mother had suggested the walk; it was always easier to spend time together when they weren't facing each other, when there was something else to do or talk about other than all the many, many things they so carefully didn't say.

Her mother squeezed her arm, a quick, almost careful touch. When had they become so careful around each other, stopped being so tactile? Her childhood had been full of easy hugs, hand holding, kisses. But now she barely touched her mother, a dutiful kiss on the cheek, the occasional quick awkward hug. When had they shifted? When her father died? After the move? Once James and his family were in the picture? 'You haven't ruined my plans at all; it's such a treat to see you. I can pop over later on; you should come too. It's Juliet's first time hosting and she's a little nervous, I think. She'd be glad to see you.'

'Did she come over yesterday?'

'Oh, yes, she and Aaron were with us all day

and Portia, Mark and the baby came for dinner, along with your grandparents and James's parents.'

'Quite the crowd.'

'As always, but we had room for one more. There's always room, Elfie.'

Elfie didn't know what to say so she didn't say anything at all. They continued in silence for a while until her mother spoke.

'When did you say your flight was?'

'The second of January. But I can find a hostel tomorrow...'

'Nonsense, of course you'll stay with us. We would love to have you.'

Elfie's instinctive reaction was to refuse but she managed to bite it back. It was one thing to stay away for work reasons, but when her mother knew full well that she wasn't working, to choose to pay to stay elsewhere was the kind of snub their already brittle relationship might never recover from. 'Thank you; that will be nice.' And maybe it really would. Her half siblings had seemed pleased to see her, even James had muttered something about the prodigal returning before handing her a coffee and offering to make her French toast.

She still felt prickly, out of shape and place in the house that had never felt like home in the four years she had lived there, but there had been no time to dwell on the past or her discomfort when Oliver decided to show her some game he had received yesterday and insisted on talking her through it in excruciating detail and Polly had brought down her sketchbook and new watercolour pencils. Elfie had found herself raising her eyebrows at her mother in some astonishment as she looked through the book. Her small sister had some talent.

The silence returned and stretched on as they walked, Elfie barely taking in the scenery, trying to think of something to say, relieved when once again her mother spoke up first.

'And where are you off to next?'

'The Caribbean again. I have a second stew post lined up, with another one starting straight after. The second stew doesn't pay as well as the Chief Stewardess role but it's half the hassle and the tips are just as good. After that, who knows?' She tried to sound as devil-may-care as she usually did, as she usually was, but for once her itinerant future didn't sound so beguiling. Didn't feel so exciting. Instead, it felt lonely. Weeks of drudgery. Yachting was a young person's game. She was getting too old for the long hours and nonstop partying.

'The Caribbean does sound appealing right

now, but it's a shame your other job has come to an end. Your posts are so clever; you have a real eye—and a way with words.'

'You follow my account?' Elfie stared at her mother in astonishment.

'Your dog nanny account? Yes. For a few months now. It was Juliet who showed it to me; she's been wanting a dog for ages and has been using your pictures to persuade Aaron.' Her mother paused and when she spoke again her voice was very carefully casual. 'You know that Juliet is our Head of Marketing now? She says you are full of flair, that you should work in social media full-time. We could do with someone with your skills.'

'I'm not going to move home and work for the family firm, Mum.' Not her home, not her family, but for once she kept that part to herself and the unsaid words weren't bitter on her tongue.

'No. I suppose not.' Another pause. 'It's your life, darling…'

'But?' Here it came. But, at the same time, Elfie couldn't help but acknowledge that she reverted to angry teenager the second she saw her mother, her skin paper-thin, every nerve on edge, every word perceived as an implied criticism.

'Not a but, more of a what. How long do you think the travelling and the short-term jobs will make you happy? I'm not criticising,' she said hurriedly, and Elfie's heart constricted. She wasn't the only one walking on eggshells here. 'You have been all round the world, seen so much, had adventures. It's just…where does it lead? Do you want to be doing this at thirty? At thirty-five?'

'Actually, I do have a plan. I was hoping I could buy the French house from you.' Elfie hadn't meant to ask so abruptly, or yet, but really, what was she waiting for? Her savings were healthy, she had a good social media presence of her own, thanks to some strategic tagging and cross posts; she could put some steady months in on charter and then head to France at the end of the season and get started. She waited for the anticipatory excitement that always filled her when she thought about owning her childhood home, but it didn't come. Instead, all she felt was the same numbness that had consumed her since last night.

'The French house? You don't have to buy it, silly girl; it's yours.'

'Mine?' It wasn't the answer she was expecting and it took Elfie a few moments to absorb it. If the house was hers then there was nothing stopping her from living her dream, nothing at all. She just needed to push away the memory of dark eyes, clever hands and a reluctantly charming smile. 'I had no idea. How, when?' Not the most articulate of responses but it wasn't every day that she found out she was a homeowner.

'As soon as I get the documents drawn up and transfer ownership. I always planned to sign it over to you. I don't visit any more, too many memories, I suppose, and it didn't seem right to take James there. But I also didn't want to burden you with any debt, so I have been renting it out as a holiday home to pay off the rest of the mortgage and it finally happened earlier this year. Don't get too excited, though. The place is a money pit. Honestly, we barely make enough on it for the repairs once the cleaning and letting costs are taken into consideration...'

'I don't want to let it. I want to live there. I want to open it as a retreat, like Papa wanted. He didn't get the chance to make his dreams come true, thanks to me. So I want to make them come true for him.'

Elfie couldn't help but see the concern in her mother's eyes. 'Like I said, Elfie, the house is yours whenever you need it, whatever you want to do with it, but are you sure it's the right place for a retreat? It's small, remember? Only three bedrooms and one of those is a boxroom. And it still gets cut off from the village whenever it floods, and the range is as temperamental as ever. As for the water pressure... I market it as bijou and rustic and price it accordingly because, no matter how charmingly I decorate it and the quality of the welcome hamper, people still like hot water upstairs and to be able to cook their meals evenly.'

'I could replace the range.'

'You could. It's cast iron and practically weighs as much as the house itself. But you'd still only be able to have two guests, even if you take the boxroom.'

'I was thinking of pods, you know, glamping pods and shepherd's huts. They're very popular.'

'You'd need a bigger cesspit,' her mother said. Her voice softened. 'How you remind me of your father.'

'What do you mean?'

'You're a dreamer too.'

'There's nothing wrong with having dreams,' she said defensively.

'Of course there isn't. I loved that about him, his ability to ignore practicalities, to conjure up his version of reality so enticingly I found my-self convinced, despite my misgivings. I certainly never meant to be married and pregnant at twenty-two, living in a rundown cottage in the middle of nowhere in a different country, but he made every moment exciting, anything possible. Of course, it wasn't all roses around the door. There were plenty of times when it snowed and the range went out and we had no hot water and I couldn't cook, when we were cut off by floods and running out of food—then he turned to me for practical solutions. And you know how terrible he was to live with when his painting wasn't working the way he wanted. It's a good thing I wasn't the same way. Can you imagine how it would have been if we'd both stamped around swearing?'

Elfie heard her mother's reminiscent laugh, the fondness in her voice with some surprise. 'You still miss him.'

'Of course I do!'

'But James is so different.'

'Elfie, it's quite possible to love two very different people. When your father was alive I could ignore all the impracticalities in our life, but once he was gone it all seemed impossible, especially with a child to take care of. I wasn't looking to replace your father, his place in my heart is his alone, but I love James just as much. I needed someone solid, someone settled, and he gave me that. I know you never took to him and I know how much my marrying him hurt you, but he has made me happy.'

'I want you to be happy,' Elfie mumbled. How had they never had this conversation before? At first she had been too young, too raw, too angry. Too guilty. And then she'd made sure she was never available for any kind of conversation, often thousands of miles away and keeping up her defences on her rare visits. 'I'm sorry.' The words were almost choked out.

'You don't have to be sorry for anything. I should apologise to you, Elfie, and I have been searching for the right moment for quite some time.' Her mother took a deep breath. 'I know how much upheaval you went through, losing your father, leaving your home, and my marriage to James must have felt very sudden. And I know that I was so busy trying to be the perfect stepmother to Juliet and Portia, to help them through the transition, that you felt neglected. I guess I thought that we were such a tight unit nothing would come between us. I was wrong and I have had to live with the consequences of that ever since. I miss you,

Elfie, every day. And I am sorry for letting you down.'

'But you didn't. I let you down. Papa died because of me. That's why I have to build his retreat, to make his dreams come true. And that's why I am so, so sorry. Can you ever forgive me?' The words tumbled out, held inside for so long.

Her mother stopped, turning to Elfie with shock on her face. 'Elfie, I don't need to forgive you; what happened was not your fault. Have you really thought that all this time? But why?'

'Because…' The whole world was swaying around her. 'I wouldn't leave him alone, even though I knew better. He went out to get away from me. I was responsible. You know this. You were right when you said I ruined everything.'

'When?' Her mother's eyes were full of shock.

'Before you married James. When you wanted me to come shopping for bridesmaids' dresses…' Elfie could remember every second of that day. How had her mother forgotten?

'That was wicked of me, but Elfie, I was talking about the times we spent with James and the girls, your refusal to be at the wedding, not your father. I should never have said it at all, but I had no idea you thought…that all this time.' And then her mother was crying, huge sobs racking the petite frame she had bequeathed to her daughter, and as Elfie allowed herself to be drawn into her mother's arms she felt the cold sting of tears on her face and realised that she, who hardly ever allowed herself to show weakness, was crying too.

# CHAPTER THIRTEEN

'So this is Scotland...what do you think?'

Xander wasn't really expecting Walter to answer, which was a good thing as Walter just cocked his head to one side and looked enquiringly up at him. They'd arrived at Glen Thorne that morning, after taking the sleeper train up from London, and were both in need of some fresh air and exercise.

The snow had melted in Buckinghamshire and London but was still thick in this corner of the Highlands. The view from the hotel grounds was stunning, with white mountains dominating the horizon in two directions, the blue of the loch ahead. Usually, Xander looked forward to his visits to the castle, found a certain amount of peace in the beautiful landscape, but his heart was heavy as he looked around.

It was four days since Elfie had sneaked out of the hotel in his absence, leaving him just a terse text. At first he had been angry, too angry to reply. If she was going to treat him with such a lack of courtesy, to act like a coward then he had misjudged her and was better off without her. Or at least that was what he tried to tell himself. Then he decided that with less than a week to go of their friendship, what did it matter when she left and threw himself into work, barely emerging from his office for forty-eight hours. But at night he could see the anguish in her stormy grey eyes as she'd told him she was doomed to ruin everything she touched, heard the urgency in her voice as she'd begged him to marry for love and he would replay the conversation, wondering where it had gone wrong, what he could have said or done to turn the direction, to convince her.

Convince her of what? That she was entitled to a happy life of her own? Allowed to love and be loved? Needed to forgive herself? Needed to find her own path rather than obsessively follow a dead man's dream? How could he convince her of those facts if he had never lived that way himself? The irony was that she'd urged the same on him. Two people who wanted more for the other than for themselves.

It was ridiculous. 'Ridiculous,' he told Walter, who was more interested in eating snow than listening to Xander. And who could blame him?

What was also ridiculous was that four days in he was missing her more than ever and being here without her just intensified the ache of loss. He'd wanted to share the journey with her, see the moment she first set foot in the castle, have her by his side when he hosted the Hogmanay party. He wanted stolen kisses in corners and walks in the snow and long, heated nights in bed. He wanted to run ideas past her and see her frown of concentration as she decided on the caption for a picture, her utter focus as she set up a photo, her laughter when she played with Walter. Her desire when their gazes locked. He had never had this connection before. Had never wanted anyone so much, enjoyed anyone's company so much. He loved everything about her. He…

Hang on. He *what*? 'People don't fall in love in just four weeks,' he told Walter and the dog grunted dismissively as if to say: *What do you know?*

'Of course they don't.' He stomped on through the snow. 'Okay, Leo always said the second he set eyes on Kate he knew that she was the one and they were married within a few months, but that is just Leo. He's impulsive; he was just lucky they worked out.'

They carried on into the woods, forging a path as they did. Xander welcomed the cold, the distraction. But, try as he might, he couldn't shut out the word spinning through his mind. *Love.*

'I can't love her. Because if I did I would have known what to say, I would have been able to make it all right. Wouldn't I?'

Was that what love was? Knowing what to say, how to make things right? Was it this hollow feeling that an essential part of him was missing? Or was it the desire to know that Elfie was safe and well, even if she was a thousand miles away, that her happiness was paramount? One thing he knew for sure was that she wasn't happy, that she'd been running away for over a decade now and her early-morning departure was just another stage in her escape from feeling anything for anyone. Including herself.

He looked at Walter. 'I think...' he said slowly. 'I think that if I thought she was genuinely happy then I could live with missing her. But she's not, is she? She doesn't know how to be. That's why I think she should know that someone is on her side. That, no matter what she says or does, she's loved unconditionally. Because she is. I do.'

Suddenly aware that Walter had wandered off and that he was standing talking to himself, he called Walter to heel and made his way back to the hotel, an imposing granite castle that had stood in this spot, repelling invaders for hundreds of years. Inside, the décor was traditional, with plenty of the family tartan, comfortable tweed and leather furniture and the odd stag's head on the wall. He'd looked into modernising it a couple of times, but the feedback had always convinced him that the guests loved it just as it was, loved stepping into a Highland fantasy.

As always, they were booked up for New Year, but the castle had plenty of public spaces and Xander had the smaller library to himself as he settled into a comfortable chair by the fire, Walter at his feet and a whisky in his hand. He stared into the flames, mind whirling. It seemed that, much as he tried to, he couldn't escape two indubitable facts. One, he loved Elfie. No matter that it seemed too soon, that he had never meant this to happen, he loved her. And, despite everything that meant, despite her absence, the knowledge warmed him through as thoroughly as the whisky. He hadn't thought love was for him, assumed himself incapable. Turned out his friends had been right all along. All he needed was the right woman. Which led him to point two. The right woman wasn't here. He had let her down and let her go. He didn't even know where she was.

He looked down at his phone. That wasn't entirely true. He could call her or text her, or he could show her how he felt. Go back to the beginning.

He looked down at Walter. 'I think I need your help.'

Walter looked up sleepily, his tail half wagging.

'If all else fails, we could make a dramatic journey to the airport, I suppose. But let's see if she responds to you.'

One thing was certain. No matter what happened with Elfie, Xander knew he couldn't allow his life to be so narrowly defined again. He was allowed to combine personal happiness along with his duty. Doing so didn't make him weak or selfish; it just made him human.

He just hoped the realisation hadn't come too late.

Elfie sat at her mother's kitchen table, only half listening to the busy chatter around her. What a different life her half siblings, no, her brother and sister, she corrected herself, lived. They had grown up in a busy home with extended family all around, so different from her isolated childhood several miles from the nearest village. She'd gone to school, of course, had friends, but she'd often been absent when her father had decided he needed a road trip, and she'd been too far out for anything but play dates scheduled in advance. She'd been a happy but solitary child, content with her own company. She'd never lost that sense of isolation even when crammed with roommates and other staff into small crew quarters on a yacht or the tiny service living space in New York penthouses, keeping something essential of herself back. But she hadn't kept anything back from Xander in the end.

Not that it had done any good. She had left and he hadn't contacted her since. She didn't blame him in the least, but she had to admit that a part of her had wished for a huge dramatic gesture, some sign that he missed her, wanted her to return. It was ridiculous; he didn't even know where she was. And surely it was better this way; she had to sort herself out before she was by any means ready to be in any kind of relationship.

Xander deserved someone without baggage or hesitations, not a half-formed girl. She repressed a sigh. She couldn't expect him to wait for her, especially after that cowardly exit and text goodbye. The best-case scenario was that he would fall in love with someone wonderful and live happily ever after. The most likely scenario was that he would marry Cressida within the year and revert to the remote Baron, striding through his estate, suppressing all emotion for duty.

Either way, she wouldn't be there, and even if it was through choice it still hurt almost unbearably. She found it hard to sleep and when she did finally drift off it was with Xander's face before her, sometimes the brown eyes soft with empathy, sometimes alight with desire, but in her nightmares they were always hard with contempt. She had been right when she'd told him that she destroyed everything; the irony was that it was a self-fulfilling prophecy. She did it to herself. And now it was too late.

The buzz of her phone interrupted her thoughts and she glanced over at the screen, noting that she had an email and a social media message notification. She hadn't posted anything over the last week, sending all the sign-in details for Walter's and the Dog Nanny accounts to the Baron Thornham marketing people, and kept away from her personal account, unable to fake a life she no longer understood. She opened the email, expecting to see a marketing message, only to let out a surprised cry as she took in the contents.

'What is it?' Her mother looked up from the other end of the table where she was giving Polly a drawing lesson. 'Is everything okay?'

'Not really. The ship I was employed on has been in an accident and needs some major repairs, so the first charter season has been cancelled and the second's in doubt. They've said if I fly over they'll see if they can get me some cover work, but...' she shrugged '...it's not easy fitting in with a crew halfway through a season and financially it's not as stable.'

'How much do you make?' James, her stepfather, asked.

'The salary isn't bad. Around two thousand pounds, sometimes more, for the six weeks, but it's the tips that make it worthwhile. I can clear three thousand pounds a week.'

James whistled. 'Nice.'

'And with very few expenses. With two seasons lined up, I was hoping to take home around forty thousand after costs.'

'For twelve weeks' work?'

She nodded. 'If I was employed the whole time. I should pick up work easily, but every day spent waiting for a vacancy is money not earned and spent on accommodation and food.' It wasn't just the lack of employment giving her pause. It was the knowledge that the thought of the forthcoming season gave her no pleasure at all. She was tired of travelling, tired of being alone. 'But I don't have anything else lined up. It's too late for the ski season now.' And she had thrown away her job at the hotel along with any chance of a future with Xander.

'You don't have to make any decisions now,' her mother said. 'You can stay here as long as you need to. Maybe we could go over to France and see if the cottage is suitable for what you're envisioning.'

'That's kind of you. I'd like that.' And she would. Maybe visiting France with her mother would help lay some ghosts. And the thought of staying here didn't feel as painful as it usually did. She and James seemed to be getting on better and she was enjoying getting to know Polly and Oliver. Her stepsisters both lived nearby and had suggested meeting for a drink, which was an unexpected and not unwelcome olive branch—and she knew she still had a long way to go repairing her relationship with her mother. None of it was easy; heading off was by far the easiest option, postponing all this family reconciliation for another time. But it was time to stop running.

And if she was staying in Surrey then maybe she could try and see Xander. Apologise. Try and explain, if she could figure out what to say.

'What are you planning to do tomorrow?' her mother asked.

'Tomorrow?'

'It's New Year's Eve.'

'Of course. I was supposed to be in Scotland.' Which meant Xander was already there. Was he missing her? For a second the realisation of all she had thrown away overwhelmed her, a physical pain. Xander had listened to her, understood her, tried to repair her and she had walked away because she was scared.

Was it too late to tell him she was sorry? That she missed him? That she wished she had made different choices?

Her phone buzzed again, a second notification. She picked it up and realised it was from the same account as the first, one she didn't recognise, and she frowned as she cautiously opened it. Unknown accounts could often mean trouble, spam if she was lucky, unwanted pictures if not. The account was named

Future Adventures and she grimaced. If this was some wellbeing site trying to persuade her to buy their visualisation techniques then it would be an instant block.

Instead of a hard sell or a picture of some male anatomy she saw Walter, wearing a bow tie made of an attractive grey and purple tartan. The caption merely said 'Missing you'. Tears welled up as she looked at the small dog, knowing Xander must have taken the photo, set up the account to send it to her.

She swiped onto the next picture. Walter again, this time next to a photo of Xander, looking absurdly young in formal dress, black tie and a kilt. 'He misses you too'. Elfie repressed a smile as her phone pinged again with a third notification. She opened it, butterflies fluttering madly. This time Walter was outside, panting by a message carved into the snow. 'We love you, Elfie'.

Elfie sat and stared at the picture, reading the words over and over. Love? After everything? As in platonic love? It was a word that could be tossed around so carelessly; she saw it all the time. Or romantic love, hearts and flowers, sweet but possibly insubstantial? Or real love, strong and deep and enduring? The kind of love that grew with time, anchoring and supportive. Because, with no surprise but more a growing awareness, she knew that she loved Xander in all three of those ways. He was her friend, he was her lover and he was her oak. Did he feel the same way?

There was only one way to find out.

'I think...' she said, still staring at the phone '...that I will be going to Scotland for New Year's Eve after all. I'd better book my train.'

It had been over twenty-four hours since Xander had sent Elfie the messages, and over twenty-four hours since she had opened them, but he hadn't heard a peep from her in all that time. Had he misjudged the situation? Did she not want to hear from him; had their time together been just a fling after all? Or had he scared her? She already found it hard to trust; had the messages sent her fleeing?

Or was she thinking about the best way to respond?

No matter which it was, the ball was in her court now. All he could do was wait and hope.

Luckily, he would be busy tonight at the annual Hogmanay party. Guests would be treated to drinks followed by a lavish five-course meal, before a ceilidh took them into the New Year. The night was packed with traditions, with Auld Lang Syne sung at midnight before one of the villagers arrived as the first footer, armed with gifts of shortbread and cake for all the guests. Like Christmas at Thornham Park, the New Year celebrations involved many return guests and the ceilidh was open to anyone from the village who wished to attend, making it a long and festive night.

As was customary, Xander was in black tie complete with kilt as he received his guests, Walter by his side, dapper in his bow tie. The ballroom was resplendent, decorated with plenty of greenery and sparkling lights, cosy seating areas in the alcoves along one side for those who would prefer not to dance. A local band played traditional folk songs as the guests mingled, champagne circulating, the villagers as dressed up as the guests, many of whom they knew from years gone by, and the two groups chatted easily as they caught up on a year's worth of news.

Xander found himself relaxing as the last of the guests entered the ballroom. He was nearly done. He had hosted a festive season on his own. The guests were happy, repeat bookings already being taken for next year, the PR and reviews positive and the staff seemed pleased. He would never have his father's hearty presence or his grandfather's easy charm, but he could be himself. He just wished he had realised that a long time ago.

He was about to step into the ballroom when he saw a last guest come hastily through the reception and turned to greet her when Walter, who had sat patiently by his side throughout the whole receiving line, gave a little high-pitched whine before hurtling along the passageway to throw himself on the distant figure. Xander was about to call him back when the figure came into view and he froze, heart thumping wildly.

Elfie. Cheeks flushed, wrapped up in her big coat, hair ruffled.

'I'm sorry I'm late.'

'What kept you?' He could feel a smile curving his mouth as she responded in kind, her smile lighting up her eyes.

'My train was late and so I missed my connection. I ended up getting changed in the loos at Edinburgh. I wasn't the only one, though.' She shrugged off her coat to reveal a black lace cocktail dress, cut low at the front, the straps encircling her arms, leaving her creamy shoulders bare. 'It was quite the party. I was almost sorry to leave.'

'Nice outfit.'

'It's my stepsister's.'

He raised his eyebrows and she laughed. 'I have a lot to tell you, but first…' Her eyes grew serious and he took her hand, not wanting anything to spoil this perfect moment.

'But first we dance.'

'In there?' She sounded a little daunted and, looking around, Xander realised that the folk music had given way to ceilidh music and the guests had started an enthusiastic Dashing White Sergeant.

'No, in here.' He pulled her into the small antechamber beside the ballroom, closing the door, although the music was still clearly audible. 'In here and like this.'

'The dancing doesn't seem to match the music,' she said as he enfolded her in his arms, swaying gently.

'We'll just have to make do. Elfie, I can't believe you're here.'

She looked up, her heart in her eyes. 'Xander, I am so sorry. I panicked and I did what I always do when I am overwhelmed; I ran.'

'My life can be a bit much. I'm often overwhelmed myself.'

'No, not by your life. That's part of you, the duty and obligation you bear. And you do it so well; that's one of the things that drew me to you. No, I was overwhelmed by you. By the way I feel for you. I had convinced myself that the only way to keep myself safe was to keep myself away from any connections. I told myself I was happier that way. And then you came along and I tore up the rule book. I let you into my life, my bed, my confidence and then I realised that I had let you into my heart and that was terrifying. Leaving you like that was wrong and I am so sorry, but I honestly thought I was doing the right thing for both of us.'

'You let me into your heart?' He needed to hear her say it and she nodded.

'I love you, Xander. I tried not to, but I just couldn't help it. I love how much you care. How you make me laugh. How you make me feel. And if it's all right with you, I would like to agree to your suggestion that we see where this thing goes. Because with you by my side I'm not afraid. Not any more.'

There. She had said it. She'd laid her heart on the line and it was up to Xander now. And even if he said he had changed his mind, even if he sent her away, she wouldn't regret any of it. Not the long journey north, not the words, not the long hard look at her life she'd used the journey to do. Because she was better for knowing him, for loving him, and how could she regret that?

'I love you too, Elfie.' It had been one thing seeing the words written down; it was another to hear them, spoken low and intimate, his voice full of sincerity and passion. 'I think I loved you from the moment I first saw you. You make me want to be better, to do better. My life isn't easy and it's not conventional, but if you could bring yourself to share it with me I would be the luckiest man alive.'

'I'm not afraid of unconventional or hard work. I would want a base, though; I've not had one for a very long time. Here or Buckinghamshire, a place to hang our pictures, to put our books, a bed only we sleep in.'

'Don't forget Walter.'

'How could I?' She could feel a small head butting her knee and leaned down to caress the silky curls. 'He's our matchmaker.'

'Yes to the base. Yes to anything you want. Just as long as you'll stay.'

'For as long as you want me,' she promised, and his eyes were tender.

'Then prepare yourself for forever.' And with that he kissed her, sweet and welcoming, a pledge of the days—and the nights—to come. Elfie sank into the kiss, into Xander, knowing that whatever happened she was no longer alone. That where Xander was, she was meant to be.

She'd spent her whole life searching for a home, yet running from any kind of commitment. But how could she regret any of it when her search had brought her here, to Xander? To a man who miraculously seemed to need her, to want her, to love her as much as she needed and wanted and loved him.

It had been a long, lonely road, but Xander's kiss promised a brighter future filled with love, happiness and laughter.

'I love you,' she whispered against his mouth and felt his answering smile.

'And I you.'

He held her tight as they moved to the music, Walter close by their sides, and as the clock struck twelve and ushered in a New Year, Elfie knew her journey had ended at last.

\* \* \* \* \*